A TIME TO BE...

By

Rosemary Hillyard

Copyright © Rosemary Hillyard 2016
This book is sold subject to the condition that it shall not, by way of trade or otherwise, be lent, resold, hired out, or otherwise circulated without the publisher's prior consent in any form of binding or cover other than that in which it is published and without a similar condition including this condition being imposed on the subsequent publisher.
The moral right of Rosemary Hillyard has been asserted.
ISBN-13: 978-1534901643
ISBN-10: 1534901647

I dedicate this book to my partner, John McGoldrick, and my lifelong friend, Marion Cattermole, with thanks for their love, support, and loyalty through good and tough times for so many years.

CONTENTS

Chapter 1 .... *1*
Chapter 2 .... *6*
Chapter 3 .... *8*
Chapter 4 .... *15*
Chapter 5 .... *24*
Chapter 6 .... *28*
Chapter 7 .... *32*
Chapter 8 .... *39*
Chapter 9 .... *48*
Chapter 10 .... *53*
Chapter 11 .... *62*
Chapter 12 .... *67*
Chapter 13 .... *72*
Chapter 14 .... *80*
Chapter 15 .... *86*
Chapter 16 .... *91*
Chapter 17 .... *95*
Chapter 18 .... *98*
Chapter 19 .... *102*
Epilogue *109*
About the Author *112*

This is a work of fiction. Names, characters, businesses, organizations, places, events and incidents either are the product of the author's imagination or are used fictitiously. Any resemblance to actual persons, living or dead, events, or locales is entirely coincidental.

Chapter 1

1960

The sky had been dark for hours now and still there was no news. The short, stocky man paced the narrow, dimly-lit corridor, anxiously waiting…

He had been at the hospital for twelve hours, unable to leave Maria on her own, although several times that friendly little blonde nurse had told him gently to go home and try not to worry, because there was nothing he could do. The baby would arrive in its own time.

Of course, he knew that, but he couldn't help worrying. Wasn't it only natural when your wife was having her first child at the age of thirty-eight?

There had been several earlier pregnancies, but she'd not been able to carry any of them longer than a few months, and both knew in their hearts that if this baby didn't live they would never have a child of their own. The doctor had warned him that she probably wouldn't have an easy time and that, whatever happened, it would be most unwise to attempt another pregnancy. So all their hopes – and Maria's prayers – were pinned on this baby...

John Carter wasn't a man much given to praying. Any notions he held of God were vague images dating back to his childhood, a distant picture at Sunday school of a holy man with limpid eyes and a saintly expression, surrounded by a pool of light. He loved his wife deeply and envied her strong faith in a real, loving God whom she worshipped with conviction and trusted implicitly. He knew how much she wished he could believe as she did, but somehow he couldn't bring a 'real' God to mind.

Now, though, as he stopped for what seemed the thousandth time at the high, narrow window at the end of the corridor overlooking the garden, he was trying with all his strength to pray to whatever deity was out there...

He stared at the wintry landscape. The leafless branches of a silver birch tree moved restlessly in the wind which whispered sadly against the glass, rattling the ill-fitting old wooden frame.

Needs fixing, his ever-practical mind told him.

A thick border of mature rhododendron bushes loomed blackly against the snow-covered ground, sparkling here and there as the light from a fitful moon struck icy patches. Beyond, a long lawn sloped steeply down to the high wall and wrought-iron gates which defined the hospital's supremacy, positioned high above the town, and, farther into the distance, points of light winked in the house windows and street lights.

They had moved to Westfield nearly twenty years ago, soon after they had married. Work had been scarce in their home town and he'd felt they would be safer there, farther out in the countryside, with the bombing raids hitting the big industrial towns so heavily.

And they'd expected babies to start arriving soon. Maria was barely nineteen, but most young couples then dreamed of finding a little home and having a couple of babies to bring up in a peaceful world...

But it was five years before peace returned to wartorn England and homes that weren't bomb-damaged were hard to find. Eventually they had scraped together enough from his shoe-repairing business (he'd been exempt from military service, much to his chagrin, because of his asthma) and Maria's nursing auxiliary work to put down a deposit on a tiny cottage. It was only a two-up, two-down with an outside toilet, but it was in the centre of Westfield and it was theirs!

They were able to turn the front room into a little shop where he could work, and he was soon getting plenty of business by recommendation from the people with money who lived on the slopes of the hill.

Through the window John could see the Victorian-style lamp-posts flanking the porch of the square, red-brick house of Sir Arthur Brown, who owned the thriving factory which turned out metal parts for almost any household appliance you cared to name.

In those days the factory was producing munitions to

help the war effort, and, although Sir Arthur was plain Mr Brown then and some way off making his first million, he was a still a greatly respected man in Westfield. Choosing John to repair all his household's boots and shoes had been quite a feather in his cap. In fact, mused John as he stared through the window, it was thanks to Sir Arthur that his business had thrived.

So, by the end of the war, they had their own home and enough money to allow Maria to give up her nursing, and they were confident the babies would follow. But five years passed, then ten, without any sign of a pregnancy. Visits to specialists always ended with the same words: 'We can't find anything wrong. Keep trying, that's all we can say.'

Until Maria turned thirty. Then the advice changed. 'We're sorry, but it seems nature decided you weren't to be parents. Best to forget about children and find other ways to fill your lives.'

But Maria wanted a child so much, and John couldn't bear to see her unhappy. And her thirty-first birthday arrived with the wonderful news that she was pregnant! Two months later she lost the baby, and, in the next five years she miscarried twice more. To have carried this baby to full term was a miracle, and John knew he ought to believe in a loving God more wholeheartedly.

A scream from the delivery room jerked him abruptly out of his reverie. Another scream, then a third... He couldn't bear it, what was happening to his beloved Maria in there?

Clenching his fists to control his emotions, he took a deep breath and moved towards the door. At that moment he heard a thin, high wail and a joyful babble of voices, and the door swung open to reveal the little blonde nurse, her face beaming.

'You can come in, Mr Carter – you've a lovely daughter!'

He crossed to the bed where Maria lay, exhausted. Her pretty, fair hair was plastered dark with sweat against the pillow, and grey shadows below her eyes marred the delicate face. But she was smiling tenderly and lying cradled in one arm was a small white-wrapped bundle.

He bent to kiss his wife and inspect the daughter for whom they had both waited so long. A tiny crumpled pink face topped with a light fuzz of fair hair was all he could see above the blanket. His throat contracted painfully and suddenly they were both crying and laughing and kissing all at the same time.

At that moment, church bells all over Westfield started ringing, pealing and crashing joyfully together.

'Happy new year, Mr and Mrs Carter,' the little nurse wished them, smiling. 'Happy 1960.'

'A new year, a new decade, and a new life for us.' John touched the baby's downy head gently. 'Welcome, Elizabeth Maria Carter!'

Chapter 2

As the bells rang out, the wrinkled papery eyelids in the face of an old man in another wing of the hospital flickered open momentarily. The slim, silver-haired woman bent forward.

'They're ringing in the new year, Edward – it's 1960.'

She gently pressed the thin hand with the almost transparent skin which lay limply on the cream blanket.

'Sure they're not ringing to mark my departure, Hetty?' he whispered with a ghost of a smile on his pale lips.

She bent closer to catch his words, but with a faint sigh the flicker of life had gone out. For a few seconds she was not sure that this was the end, and waited to hear him speak again.

'I'm sorry, madam.'

The young doctor touched her shoulder hesitantly. He hated such moments. He had gone into medicine in the belief that he could save people's lives and make them well again. Death meant he had failed in this task.

Henrietta Kerbridge bent over the old man, calm and peaceful now that his suffering was over. She lightly touched the scars that ran down one side of his face, then pressed a kiss on his white forehead and whispered so low that the doctor could not hear her words.

'Goodbye, Edward, my dearest love, until we meet again.'

Her violet-blue eyes were bright with unshed tears as she rose. But her natural poise and elegance did not desert her, even in her grief.

With calm dignity, she shook the doctor's hand, thanked him for his care of Edward, and turned to walk away. He watched her until she reached the double doors at the far end of the long ward. Her head held high, her slim back erect, her stride that of a much younger woman, she made an elegant picture.

'Now that's what I call a lady,' he said to himself in admiration as the doors swung open, then closed behind her. 'A real lady…'

Chapter 3

'Are you sure it's wise to go out so soon?' John watched his wife anxiously as she buttoned her coat and tidied her hair in front of the hall mirror.

'John, dear, I need some fresh air and so does Elizabeth. I've had lots of rest in the last three weeks, and the doctors wouldn't have let us come home if they hadn't been sure we were both fine. Please stop worrying. I won't stay out long, but I want to take Elizabeth to the church to offer a prayer of thanks for her safe delivery.'

John hugged Maria and planted a kiss on her forehead.

'Okay, you win. I know it's no use arguing with you when you've made up your mind. But keep on the move, won't you? Although it's brighter today, there's still quite a cold wind, and I'd hate either of my girls to catch a chill!'

Maria grinned at him as she pulled a blue woollen hat firmly down over her ears, wound a matching fringed scarf round her neck, and picked up her gloves.

'There, is that better? I won't catch cold now. I'll be warm as toast!'

Elizabeth was already asleep, tucked firmly in the blankets in her pram, her pink knitted bonnet and one white-mittened tiny fist peeping above the coverlet.

Maria pushed the pram proudly along the street towards St Benedict's. It wasn't the nearest church to their home – that was the modern, yellow-brick St John the Baptist round the corner – but Maria preferred the more traditional services at St Benedict's, even though it meant a walk of half a mile or so. The people there were so friendly, too, and she was looking forward to taking Elizabeth with her. The vicar welcomed children, no matter how young, and she was sure he would be delighted to arrange the baby's baptism.

Today, she'd be even more glad to reach the church. John had been right – the wind was cold – and she walked briskly, barely glancing at the front gardens of the houses she passed, not stopping as she usually did to admire a fine shrub or border. She did notice, however, that there was still an odd patch of snow here and there which the wintry rays of sun hadn't reached.

As she turned thankfully under the lychgate at the entrance to the churchyard, and started pushing the pram along the stone-flagged path between the gravestones, she caught a snatch of organ music and realised that she wouldn't have the church to herself.

Still, if it was old Mr Johnson practising for next Sunday's services, he wouldn't mind at all if she wandered round the church, running her fingers over the beautiful carved wooden choirstalls and reading the marble tablets set high in the walls. She liked to sit quietly in her favourite pew, imagining what the people commemorated in those tablets looked like and the kind of lives they led. What must it have been like to have lived in those long-ago days?

John teased her about what he called her 'romantic fancies', but Maria hoped that Elizabeth, as she grew up, would share her passion for the past. And, of course, her religious beliefs. If she set the foundations for her daughter this early, well, who knew...?

But, as she pushed open the heavy dark oak door and manoeuvred the pram, with some difficulty, down the broad stone step just inside, she realised that Mr Johnson wasn't practising: a funeral service was in progress. An oak coffin topped with a wreath of evergreens and white chrysanthemums lay on a stand before the altar, and in the front two pews stood a small, sombrely dressed group of people, singing the final verse of 'Abide With Me'.

Maria hesitated, feeling like an intruder. But it was too cold to wait outside, and she didn't want to walk home without offering her thanks to God for the baby, so she parked the pram at the back of the church and slipped into the last pew as the vicar climbed the steps of the pulpit to begin his address.

'Let us give thanks for the life of Edward Oscar Dinsdale...'

Maria started. Where had she heard that name before?

'...A very brave man, a man who risked his life in trying to save others...' the vicar was continuing. And suddenly Maria remembered where she had seen that name; on the white marble tablet next to the special memorial window in the side chapel. A whole family of Dinsdales was listed on that marble, all killed in a terrible fire at the beginning of the century.

Lost in her reverie, Maria didn't notice that the vicar had ended his address and left the pulpit until the movement of the pallbearers caught her eye as they lifted the coffin carefully onto their shoulders and began walking slowly down the main aisle towards her. The small group of mourners followed.

She bowed her head in respect as the coffin passed her, then glanced up to be faced with the most startlingly vivid pair of violet-blue eyes she had ever seen. Their owner wasn't a young woman – about seventy, Maria judged – but she was still upright, slender and elegant in a neat grey suit and tiny black hat with a discreet feather curled along one side, topping a small heart-shaped face with silver hair brushed smoothly underneath.

The woman smiled at her and Maria, realising that she had been staring, flushed as she smiled back apologetically.

She waited until the group of mourners had left the church, then knelt to offer her prayer of thanks for the safe delivery of Elizabeth.

After a few minutes, she rose, checked to see that the baby was still sleeping soundly, then made her way to the side chapel. She was right – there, on the white marble tablet next to the memorial window, were listed the members of the Dinsdale family who had lost their lives in a fire which had destroyed their home in June 1908.

Helen, widow of Edward Samuel, aged eighty-four; her son, Samuel, aged fifty-eight, and his wife, Anne, forty-five; their children...

'Did you know Mr Dinsdale?'

The soft voice made Maria start. She had been so deep in concentration that she hadn't heard anyone enter the church, and she swung round sharply.

'I'm so sorry, my dear. I didn't mean to startle you.'

For the second time she found herself looking into those bright violet-blue eyes, which had a hint of enquiry in them now.

'I thought perhaps you'd known Mr Dinsdale... your face is familiar, but I'm sorry I can't place you at the moment...' The musical voice tailed off in a question.

'No, no, I didn't know him.'

Maria explained her reason for visiting the church and her interest in the old families of the area.

'If you would like to join us for refreshments, you would be most welcome.'

'It's very kind of you, but I must get home soon, my husband will be worrying about me being out for so long in the cold with the baby.'

'Ah, yes, of course. What a beautiful baby she is... takes after you, I think. Well, I'd better join the others. My apologies again, my dear, for startling you. Strange. I'm sure we've met before somewhere, perhaps many years ago...'

She held out her hand and smiled again.

'How rude of me, I forgot to introduce myself. Henrietta Kerbridge… although that's such a mouthful, my friends usually call me Hetty.'

'Maria Carter… and my daughter, Elizabeth.'

Hetty Kerbridge hesitated for another moment, as though trying to recall something, then moved away, and, as she reached the main door of the church, lifted her hand and waved goodbye.

Maria followed more slowly, a little puzzled. The stranger had seemed so sure that they had met before, but she was equally sure they couldn't have done so. She would have remembered those most unusual eyes…

With difficulty, Maria manoeuvred the pram up the step into the porch. As she struggled, the pram bounced and Elizabeth woke and started to cry. Her mother made soothing noises, but the indignant baby refused to respond. Walking briskly down the path made no difference; the crying grew louder.

'Okay, out you come, just for a couple of minutes.'

Rocking Elizabeth in her arms quietened the crying to sobs. The funeral party was moving away in two black cars, leaving the raw new grave just a few yards away from the main path.

Maria walked over to it and stood quietly offering a prayer for the repose of the old man's soul. She held Elizabeth tightly in her arms as she looked down at the freshly turned soil, and suddenly felt completely at peace. The baby had stopped crying and seemed to be staring into the distance.

The wind caught at Maria, but she didn't notice. A few dry leaves rustled and swirled in a giddy dance on the gravel path nearby.

Suddenly, she came to – it was cold and a light drizzle was starting. It stung her face and reminded her that her newborn daughter shouldn't be kept out in such weather.

Shivering, Maria clutched Elizabeth more closely to her, and, turning sharply away, she hurried to the pram parked near the church gate. The baby, peaceful now, still seemed to be smiling secretly to herself…

Chapter 4

1980

Elizabeth walked slowly along the gravel path between the trees. The cold air stung her cheeks and she pushed her hands deeper into her pockets, but she couldn't turn back – not yet. It was so beautiful and so quiet.

Heavy frost lay on every leaf, rimming each one with a delicate edge of sparkling white, lifting each shape to stand proud of its neighbours. Conifers, tall and stately, took on even more dignity with their white mantle. The leafless deciduous trees stood gaunt and ghostly against the colourless sky, while at ground level the tiniest plant, the most insignificant weed, were transformed into things of great beauty.

She stopped to admire the frozen flowers of a winter jasmine, the pale yellow dainty petals sharp and clear under their icy jackets, frozen in gently arching flight above a low-spreading juniper. A flash of colour caught her eye and she bent to find a cluster of crocuses, bravely blooming yellow and lilac in a hollow beneath one of the juniper's spreading branches, warmed and sheltered from the frost.

The ice on the lake to her left cracked a little as the pale sun shafted across it. A gentle scratching sound in the shrubs to her right made her turn her head, and a startled moorhen scuttled away to safety beneath a stiffly flowering mound of winter heather. Otherwise, there was silence.

Elizabeth straightened up, closed her eyes, and filled her lungs with a breath of freezing air. She let it out slowly. Her breath hung steamily in the still air and she smiled and stretched her arms above her head. She hadn't felt so relaxed in ages.

That leaden depression, the restlessness, the vague frustrations, had slipped away and, cold as she was, she didn't mind. She welcomed the sharpness, the bite of the cold, clearing her head. She enjoyed being on her own like this for a few hours. It gave her time to think, and to fantasise.

From a tiny girl, Elizabeth had loved to play out fantasies. Her dolls became characters in the fairytales her parents read to her. And, as soon as she could put a few words together on paper, she began writing her own fantastic stories peopled with princesses – golden-haired and green-eyed like herself, dragons, monsters, and animals who could speak.

She had grown up a quiet, introverted child with few friends. She wasn't unpopular – most people who met this polite, reserved little girl liked her – but she preferred her own company to that of other people.

Except for her parents and her grandmother – she was very fond of the little old lady who told her fascinating stories of her childhood in the early years of the century.

Elizabeth developed a passion for history: not the dull, dry lists of facts so beloved by history teachers, but a fascination with people of the past. She wanted to know how they lived, what they thought, how they spent their days – and, perhaps because it was an era her grandmother had lived through and remembered clearly, the Edwardian age exerted a particular fascination on the impressionable little girl.

Her behaviour worried John at times.

'Surely it isn't natural for a young girl to spend so much time delving into history books and reading about the past?' he asked Maria, concerned. 'Shouldn't she be out and about having fun with friends of her own age?'

'Don't worry about her, John,' his wife reassured him. 'She's like me in that respect. You know how much pleasure I've always had from books, and she's quiet, like me. I enjoy my own company, or being with just the two of you, and I'm pleased she's such a loving daughter. And your mother is delighted to see her so often. Not many girls would bother with an old lady.'

It was true. The old lady did enjoy the frequent visits from her granddaughter. And Elizabeth enjoyed them just as much.

She was allowed to dig into the boxes of long dresses, skirts, blouses, and hats her grandmother had so carefully stored from her girlhood, and try on whichever took her fancy. She would flounce in front of the long wardrobe mirror, turning this way and that, nodding and smiling at her reflection, and her grandmother would watch her, laughing at the little actress affectionately.

As Elizabeth grew older, she listened carefully to the stories the old lady told her of her youth, asking eagerly for details. The crumpled little figure in the high-backed armchair would grow young and supple again as she relived the past. The hesitant throaty voice would sound carefree and girlish, and Elizabeth noticed that sometimes Alice Carter would slip into the present tense and talk to people she seemed to think were in the room with them.

As the daylight faded and the room grew dim, Elizabeth fancied she could see shadowy figures in the twilight and, although she knew it was only her vivid imagination, she enjoyed pretending to her grandmother that she believed they were real people, too.

She never grew out of that passion for dressing up, and, now that she was a young woman herself, her grandmother's Edwardian clothes fitted her perfectly. She preferred wearing the high-necked cotton blouses with the 'leg of mutton' sleeves and the long serge and woollen skirts instead of the jeans, tee-shirts, and trousers chosen by her contemporaries.

Even the large hats with their floppy brims and ribbons, and the straw boaters which had been her grandfather's, suited Elizabeth's blonde colouring and framed her delicate features attractively.

'You may wear anything you choose,' her

grandmother said fondly. But Elizabeth rarely borrowed the stiff straw boaters which were such precious mementoes to Alice of the handsome young husband who had been killed in 1917, several months before her son, John, had been born.

The skirts and blouses, though, she wore frequently. She found them practical, flattering and warm. Who wanted to wear a short skirt in such cold weather as it was today? And she was a girl who enjoyed feeling feminine, so she rarely wore trousers.

She liked wearing her hair long as well, not worrying whether fashion dictated otherwise. Her father had always liked Elizabeth's hair long, just like her mother's. Maria's hair had faded now that she was nearly sixty, but in her youth it had been the colour of a sunlit cornfield, and her daughter had inherited this.

Elizabeth found her long hair easy to manage if she braided it or tied it back with a ribbon as she had today. Its blondeness contrasted attractively with the dark green knitted beret she had pulled on for warmth. The dark brown serge skirt and high-necked white cotton blouse she was wearing were from her grandmother's wardrobe and went well, despite their age, with a new camel jumper which was long enough to keep her hips warm, and nut brown leather boots. The emerald green scarf and matching gloves added bright splashes to the plain outfit and brought out the colour of her eyes. Altogether she made a pleasing picture if there had been anyone in the vicinity to admire her.

But there was no one. It seemed to Elizabeth she was in another world – a world of coldness, and sharpness, and incredible clarity. Her senses seemed heightened by the cold crispness, and she was free to imagine herself anywhere, as anybody, in any time she chose...

It was good to get away from them all for a while, her parents and Ben. It wasn't that she didn't love them: how could she not? They all cared about her so much. But that was the trouble – her parents worried and cosseted and fussed over her as though she were still the little girl they had waited for, for so long... and Ben was just the same.

Dear Ben. She felt a little guilty about her thoughts towards him. After all, he was devoted to her. He'd been in love with her ever since, as a young lad, he'd started bringing the shoes from Sir Arthur's mansion to her father's shop to be mended. She smiled to herself as she remembered the shy little girl she had been then, hiding behind her mother's skirts whenever anyone spoke to her. And Ben had become her best friend and champion, fighting her battles for her, wiping away her tears when the rougher boys had teased her and pulled her long blonde plaits.

Her parents had become so fond of him that they regarded him as the son they could never have, and from the earliest days they seemed to take it for granted that their precious Elizabeth would marry the quiet, reliable Ben.

'Good solid stock, that lad,' her father, John Carter, had commented often, drawing on his pipe as he nodded his head approvingly. 'You'd go a long way before you found another so dependable.'

And, of course, Ben had done the right thing, formally asking John for her hand as though the answer weren't a foregone conclusion. Although she was only nineteen, her parents had agreed willingly. After all, Maria had been the same age when she and John had married.

'And if you two are half as happy as we've been over all these years, you'll have a good life,' John had said, smiling tenderly at his beloved wife.

Elizabeth had been happy to fall in with their wishes. She was very fond of Ben and she felt safe with him. But he wasn't, well, very exciting. In fact, she could only describe him as medium – medium height, medium build, medium brown hair, medium blue eyes – and completely predictable. Here she was, barely a year later, finding life as a married woman… dull. Yes, that was the word for it. Dull – but at least not today.

Today was hers, to do exactly as she liked with. Today she was no longer Elizabeth Croft, a rather bored young housewife. Today she was… a princess? No, she had outgrown that fantasy when she grew old enough to realise that fairytale princesses also lived boring lives, having everything done for them.

Today she was… a sparkling young Edwardian, living in the age of fun, and colour, and gaiety, dancing into the early hours without a care in the world. And she began waltzing happily, holding her long skirt daintily with one hand as though it were a floating ballgown.

A gleam of gold in the lake brought her out of her reverie. She moved to the edge of the ice and bent to see what had caught her attention.

'Oh, you poor thing!'

A carp was caught in the reeds in the frozen water, its tail twisting frantically as it tried to free itself. Elizabeth leaned over, but couldn't reach, so looked around for a stick.

A conifer branch lay a few feet away in the undergrowth. She grabbed it and stepped carefully onto a boulder which had slipped from the rocky cliff behind into the water and was now jutting a few inches above the ice.

She bent, tucking her long woollen skirt firmly between her knees as she did so. For once, dislike them though she did, she wished she were wearing trousers for their practicality.

She swept the whippy branch across the ice close to the trapped fish. Although the ice was thin at the edges, Elizabeth had to sweep the branch several times across the surface before it broke and the carp fluttered down, shuddered, and vanished.

She peered down in an attempt to see if the fish was all right, but the water was too dark for her to see anything in its depths.

A shadow seemed to fall across the lake and Elizabeth looked up quickly. The sun had stopped shining: the silence, no longer friendly and welcoming, seemed eerie and full of foreboding.

A wind had sprung up and wispy shreds of grey clouds were scudding by, throwing dark shadows across the ice. Alarmed, Elizabeth swung round quickly, ready to hurry home. But her feet slipped on the frosty boulder and she overbalanced. With a frightened scream, she fell backwards into the lake, striking her head sharply on the ice…

At that moment a large black dog, barking wildly, came hurtling out of a nearby copse, followed by a black-garbed man on a huge chestnut horse.

'Jasper, come here! Jasper!'

The rider reined in his horse and called again to the big black Labrador. But the dog took no notice. He continued to sniff at something lying at the edge of the lake.

'What is it, boy? What have you found?'

He trotted towards the dog, then pulled up sharply and leaped off his horse as he realised that there, lying half-in and half-out of the freezing water, was the slight figure of an unconscious woman. She was lying perfectly still and her face was white.

He stepped into the shallow water and lifted her carefully. Her beret had fallen off and her long blonde hair streamed down as he set her across his horse's back, swung himself up behind her, called to the dog, and rode away.

Chapter 5

1908

Elizabeth was cold, so very cold. It was such an effort to open her eyes: her eyelids felt so heavy. She felt as though she were dragging herself up from the bottom of a very dark, deep pool.

With a herculean effort she dragged open her eyes. Only a swimming greyness met her sight. Her eyes couldn't focus and she closed them again…

The woman in the corner near the fire put down her sewing and moved over to the bed.

Poor girl, she thought. *Such a nasty accident. She's going to have quite a sore head when she wakes up.*

Tutting to herself, she tucked the bedclothes in more firmly and smoothed the wet fair hair on the pillow. As she did so, the eyelids fluttered again and she was met by a bright green pair of startled eyes…

Elizabeth stared, frightened, at the strange woman

looking down at her, framed by the dark wooden slats and heavy flowered curtains of a four-poster bed. She struggled to sit up but fell back on the pillows with a moan.

'Hush, child, it's all right. You're safe here, don't worry.'

She focussed on the plump, motherly figure bending smilingly over her, and her dry lips formed the question, 'Where am I?'

'You're at Highwood Hall, my dear, quite safe. You fell in the lake and Mr Edward found you and brought you back here to rest. The doctor will be here soon to take a look at you, and I'm sure you'll be fine in a few days.'

She smiled reassuringly at Elizabeth.

'But my family will be worried if I don't return home soon.'

Elizabeth tried to sit up again, but the motherly face and the flowered curtains framing it swam confusingly together and she abandoned the attempt.

'Please don't worry, my dear. As soon as you feel well enough, Higgins will take you home in the trap. Tell me where you live and I'll see that a note is taken to your mother right away.'

'I can't remember where I live… I can't remember anything, not even my name.' The green eyes filled with fear and tears threatened to spill over.

'When I took your wet clothes to the scullery to be cleaned and pressed, I found this little pocketbook in your skirt pocket. Do you recognise it?'

The women held out a faded brown leather purse

with a notebook and pencil attached. Elizabeth looked doubtful.

'I'm not sure. But if it was in my pocket, it must be mine. Is there anything inside?'

The woman opened the notebook. Inside the cover was a neatly printed name.

'Elizabeth Carter,' she read aloud. 'Is that your name?'

Elizabeth tried it a few times. It had a familiar sound, but she couldn't be sure. Her head hurt too much and trying to concentrate was difficult. Her brain felt fuzzy round the edges.

'It might be my name,' she said uncertainly.

At that moment there was a diffident tap on the door and a young girl's head peered nervously round it.

'Here's the doctor, Mrs Lane.'

'Well, bring him in, Polly, don't keep him standing out there.'

A large jovial man with bushy side-whiskers loomed in front of Elizabeth's face.

'Well, young lady, what happened to you then?'

'I can't remember. All I know is that I woke up in this strange bed a few minutes ago and my head hurts terribly. I don't even know who I am!'

This last sentence was cried with such anguish that little Polly, who had been listening in the background, her eyes round with amazement at this unusual turn of events, burst into noisy sobs.

'Oh, the poor dear, not even knowing 'oo she is!'

The housekeeper shook the young girl's shoulders exasperatedly.

'For goodness' sake, be quiet, Polly, and go downstairs at once. There's a lot to be done for Lady Dinsdale's dinner this evening, and you should be helping Cook.'

Snuffling into the corner of her none-too-clean apron, the little maid did as she was told.

The doctor straightened up from examining Elizabeth and patted her shoulder.

'I don't think there's too much wrong with you, young lady, except for that bump on the head. You'll have a headache for a while, and I should stay in bed until that goes away in case you feel faint. Don't worry about your memory. We often find people can't remember things after accidents like yours, but everything soon returns to normal as they start to recover. Make the most of being waited on for a day or two by Mrs Lane. That's quite a treat – I wouldn't mind being spoiled for a few days by her myself!'

'Go on with you, doctor!'

The plump face flushed rosy with pleasure at the compliment as the housekeeper turned to Elizabeth.

'I'll just show the doctor out, my dear, and then I'll be back to sit with you again if you'd like me to.'

'That's quite all right, Mrs Lane. I feel sleepy again and I'd like to rest for a while, then perhaps I'll feel better and remember who I am.'

The pale face smiled faintly and the eyelids drooped over the bright green eyes as the doctor and housekeeper quietly left the room.

Chapter 6

Elizabeth slept soundly for several hours. When she awoke, the heavy deep blue velvet curtains had been drawn across the tall windows to shut out the night, and the room was quiet except for the comforting sound of the fire crackling in the huge marble hearth.

She lay still for several moments, enjoying the flickering pattern of the firelight across the oak-panelled walls.

Then she turned her head slowly from side to side. *Good*, she thought, her head felt much better: the awful throbbing headache had subsided into a dull, heavy feeling which allowed her to take in her surroundings and enabled her to begin thinking about what had happened and how she had arrived in this unfamiliar house.

Not that her thoughts took her very far. The headache was much better, but the block in her memory remained. Try as she might, she could recall nothing of what had happened, nor, she realised with panic, of her life up to that point. Worried and upset, she sat up and reached for the little pocketbook which the housekeeper had left on the bedside table.

As she did so, the door opened, and, startled by the movement, Elizabeth swung round, dropping the notebook, which slipped to the floor.

'I'm so sorry, I didn't mean to frighten you. I thought you'd still be sleeping.'

As the speaker moved to the foot of her bed, all thought of retrieving the fallen book left Elizabeth's mind. Blotting out the firelight on the panelling was a tall, very dark-haired man who was smiling at her with the most amazing deep brown eyes… so dark were they that they appeared almost black, and Elizabeth, staring into them, felt as though she were falling, falling into deep, dark, fathomless water…

'Careful, you shouldn't be sitting up yet.'

Stunned by her reaction to him, Elizabeth had turned so pale that that the stranger had rushed forward and grasped her shoulders to prevent her falling from the bed. Solicitously, he bent over her, and once again she found herself helplessly drawn by those incredible eyes as he gently laid her back against the pillow. For a long moment the two gazed at each other, he struck by the bright green eyes staring with a feverish light into his face, she equally amazed by the unusual dark brown eyes of this very handsome man.

He recovered his composure first and sat down in the high-backed carved chair near the bed.

'How are you feeling now?' he asked her gently.

Elizabeth, blushing at her discomposure, pulled the bedclothes around her shoulders, feeling naked despite the high-necked nightdress of starched white cotton she was wearing.

'Er, well, better, I think. My head still feels odd, but it doesn't ache, well, not as much,' she mumbled in an embarrassed tone. 'But I don't know how I got here, or anything...'

'Let me explain what happened. My name is Edward Dinsdale and my family owns Highwood Hall and several farms around here.

'I was riding around the estate, visiting the tenants to discuss their problems, and one told me that the fence at the farthest point of our land beyond the lake had broken down and his sheep were wandering. He'd made a temporary repair, but was concerned that it wouldn't last long.

'Reassuring him that I would look at it straight away, I rode towards the lake, with my Labrador, Jasper, running alongside me. As we neared the lake, Jasper suddenly began barking furiously and raced ahead of me through the trees. I called him back, afraid that he would run onto the lake and fall though the ice, as the sunshine today was starting a thaw.

'What's the matter, can you remember now?'

Elizabeth had flung her hand over her mouth in an agitated gesture.

'I remember bending down to free a fish which had become trapped in the ice,' she said. 'Then everything goes black and I feel I'm falling!'

Her voice rose shrilly and, to her horror, she felt

hot tears pricking her eyes. Her throat constricted as she battled not to cry, but it was no use. The tears overflowed, coursing down her pale, stricken face, and Edward, greatly moved by her anguish, gathered her into his arms and rocked her as gently as though she had been a baby.

He smoothed her hair and patted her back, murmuring soothing words as she sobbed into his chest all her fear and pain and distress. At last, totally spent, Elizabeth's body relaxed in his arms, and Edward could tell from her regular breathing that she had dropped off to sleep again. Gently, he laid her back on her pillows and tiptoed from the room.

Chapter 7

Elizabeth woke with a start. The dark blue curtains were being opened and a shaft of bright sunlight flooded the room.

'You've slept the clock round, my dear,' said a motherly voice, 'and I'm sure it's done you the power of good after that nasty fall you took yesterday. How are you feeling this morning?'

A plump, cheerful face appeared before her.

'Very much better, thank you.'

Elizabeth smiled and stretched her arms above her head.

'I think I'd like to get up. It looks such a beautiful morning.'

'Are you sure you feel well enough?'

The housekeeper looked anxiously at her, but seemed reassured when Elizabeth smiled again and nodded her head.

'I'm not one for staying in bed when the weather's

lovely. I itch to get out of doors and enjoy the fresh air and sunshine.'

'Good. It sounds as though your memory's returning, too. At least you know what you like. Can you remember who you are and where you live?'

There was silence for several minutes as Elizabeth racked her brain. Then she shook her head slowly.

'No, I can't remember anything... except a tall, dark man...' She felt her face grow warm as she recalled the feeling of strong masculine arms holding her close – the arms of a stranger...

'That was Mr Edward,' the motherly woman said. 'He found you after his dog, Jasper, alerted him, and was so concerned about your accident that he popped in to see if you were all right. I can't say I approve of him coming into your bedroom; it's not decent, with you in bed and in only a nightdress, but well, that's Mr Edward all over. Doesn't hold with convention, that one.'

She shook her head and frowned, and Elizabeth tried hard to keep her face straight. The plump little woman sounded so straitlaced. What a funny, old-fashioned comment. Anyone would think she was back in Victorian days instead of 1980! And this nightdress she spoke of was hardly a flimsy, see-through garment: thick, serviceable cotton with a high neck and down to her ankles – who was likely to find her desirable in that?

'What are you prattling on about now, Gladys Lane?'

A deep masculine voice spoke with mock severity from the doorway.

Neither woman had heard the door open, and a flushed Mrs Lane swung round from the bed where she had been plumping up Elizabeth's pillows to enable her to sit up more comfortably.

'Mr Edward! I didn't hear you come in.' She pushed a stray strand of hair back into her tight bun and smoothed her immaculate white apron over her black dress in an agitated movement.

'No, Gladys, I know you didn't, because you were talking about me. If you're not careful you'll be out, bag and baggage, and where would you go at your great age? No one would have you!'

The owner of the deep voice advanced into the room, grinning wickedly, then laughed outright at the shocked expression on the little housekeeper's face.

'Don't worry, Gladys, I'm only teasing you. We couldn't manage this great barn of a place without you keeping all the staff in line. Highwood Hall would soon fall apart without you ruling it with a rod of iron, and then where would the Dinsdales be? The end of the clan, ruination of one of the oldest families in Britain...'

'Go on with you, Mr Edward. The Dinsdale family wouldn't collapse that easily. Generations of you have come and gone, through wars and famines and goodness knows what else, and Dinsdales have been in this house for centuries and will be for many more centuries to come.

'But I'll thank you not to call me Gladys. You know I don't like it, even though it was my dear mother's name and her mother's before her. Mrs Lane sounds much more dignified. What if young

Polly should hear you? I'm hard-pressed as it is to keep her in line, without her sniggering behind my back and telling all the others below stairs my name's Gladys!'

'The day you can't keep a slip of a girl – or a stable lad, for that matter – in line, Mrs Lane, will be the day the world ends,' Edward said firmly, and Elizabeth heard the admiration and warm affection in his voice. 'And you know I only use your Christian name in private. It's because I'm so fond of you, you know. I can't remember a time when you weren't here, running this house so efficiently, and I don't want to think of you ever leaving.'

He put an arm round the little woman and squeezed her middle affectionately. She pulled away and walked swiftly to the door.

'The day I do that'll be feet first, Mr Edward, and you know it. And don't tire this young lady out with your wild notions: she's not right yet, not by a long chalk. And I'll say it again, even if you are the master of the house, it's not seemly for you to be in a lady's bedroom, with her in a state of undress, and sitting on her bed and all, it's not decent!'

'Mrs Lane! Are you telling me she has nothing on at all?'

But only the slam of the door answered him as Edward grinned down at Elizabeth and she laughed in return.

'Are you really feeling better today?' he asked her gently. She flushed as her eyes met his dark brown ones and hastily lowered her gaze.

'Yes, much better, thank you,' she mumbled. 'But I

feel a bit embarrassed about Mrs Lane's comments…'

'Oh, don't worry about her, she's getting on a bit and is rather straitlaced, I'm afraid. Still, it's not surprising, I suppose. She must have been born early in the old queen's reign. I don't know her age, it's a state secret, I think, but she's been with us nearly forty years and thinks the Victorian age is still with us. She seems to forget we're almost a decade into the twentieth century. And I hope you're not one of those frightful suffragettes, are you?'

He laughed as he leaned over to ask the question.

'What's the matter? Are you feeling ill again?' His eyes darkened with concern as her face had paled and she was staring up at him with a look he would have described as terror.

'Elizabeth, what is it? What have I said to alarm you so?'

Her mind was grappling furiously with the words he had spoken. 'Suffragettes? The old queen's reign? A decade into the twentieth century?'

She had not realised she had spoken aloud until he grabbed her cold hands.

'Forgive me, I shouldn't have prattled on so, you're still feeling too ill to remember, aren't you? I'm sorry, did the mention of suffragettes upset you? You don't agree with what they want, is that the case?'

'Edward, I don't understand. Is this a game of some kind? This house, the servants, the old-fashioned clothes you're wearing, it's all like a stage play, just as though you've all stepped out of the Victorian age. What's it all about?'

'We're not all that old-fashioned. Granted, Mrs Lane is a bit behind the times, I've already explained that. But I've got a motor now and I go up to London in that instead of using the old trap. And Hetty would be most put out if she heard you. She prides herself on always being in the very latest mode!'

He lapsed into silence, surprised and a little annoyed by her words.

Elizabeth was still battling with her thoughts. They didn't make sense, and her head was beginning to ache again.

'I'm sorry, I didn't mean to offend you,' she said carefully. 'Perhaps my head is still suffering from that bang yesterday, but what you're saying doesn't make any kind of sense to me. What's so unusual about owning a car? Most people do. And suffragettes are people in the history books to me. No one takes much notice of all that fuss today, do they? After all, we've had the vote for two generations or more, which is only right, as men and women are equal. Surely you agree with that?'

She stopped, because he was staring at her as though she had two heads.

'I think you're right, that bang on your head must have done more harm than the doctor thought. Just what date do you think this is?'

'Well, I'm not sure exactly. I'm never very good at remembering dates. But it's wintertime, February or March, isn't it?'

'Yes, today's March 2nd. But what year is it?'

He was watching her so closely, with such a

strange expression, that she was suddenly wary of giving the answer she believed to be true, 1980.

'I, er, can't remember,' she said hesitantly.

'Give me a minute and I'll prove you're talking absolute nonsense.' He flung over his shoulder as he strode from the room. He was back very quickly with a newspaper which he dropped on the bed.

'There, that's today's paper that I was reading over breakfast. See the date?'

Elizabeth felt sick. She stared down at a copy of 'The Times' which to her eyes came from an archive. She had seen such copies before. They were all the rage. People paid hugely inflated prices for a copy of the paper printed on their birthdays or gave them to friends as an unusual gift.

But this newspaper bore the marks of having been read thoroughly at the breakfast table. Creased, folded unevenly, a smear of orange marmalade across the front page, it bore the date Monday, March 2nd, 1908.

Chapter 8

Faced with the dramatic piece of information she had just received, that somehow she had been transported suddenly seventy-two years into the past, Elizabeth could think of no explanation. The most likely one was that she was in a most incredibly vivid dream, brought on by her fascination with the Edwardian era and her desire to be more intimately involved with that time.

Thankfully, she was saved from the necessity to make any more comments by a tap on the door and the appearance of a slim young woman wearing a white starched cap and carrying a pile of clothes. Seeing Edward, she stopped in some confusion and blushed.

'Excuse me, sir, but the mistress asked me to come up and help the young lady to dress. But of course I wouldn't have come in if I'd known you were here.'

'That's all right, Rose. Come in. Elizabeth will appreciate your help, I'm sure.'

Edward left the room with a parting comment over his shoulder.

'I'll see you later, then, when you've met Mama and the rest of the clan.'

Rose laid the armful of garments she was carrying on the bed.

'Miss Henrietta thought some of her clothes might fit you, miss, so perhaps you'd like to choose something before you wash and then I'll help you dress. Your own clothes were so wet and muddy that they need to be cleaned and pressed before you can wear them again.'

'Who's Miss Henrietta?' Elizabeth asked as she pushed back the sheets and slid her feet into the slippers the maid had placed for her by the bed.

Helping her into a warm robe, Rose answered: 'She's Mr Dinsdale's ward and god-daughter. She's lived here since she was a little girl because her parents, who were close friends of the Dinsdales, were killed in a tragic boating accident.

'Of course, that was before I came here to be parlourmaid, but when Miss Henrietta turned eighteen last summer I was made her ladies' maid. She's a lovely young lady, miss, and just like one of the family. Well, of course, she will be a Dinsdale soon, when she weds Mr Edward.'

The young woman spoke as proudly as if she were talking about her own daughter, and Elizabeth smiled.

'You sound very fond of Miss Henrietta.'

'Oh, I am, miss. You'll like her, too, everybody does. And all the family are lovely. They've all been so kind to me.'

Elizabeth soon discovered that she had one thing

in common with the unknown Henrietta. They were the same size. All the clothes Rose had brought in fitted her perfectly.

Half an hour later she was ready to meet the family who had taken her in. She stood for a few moments appraising herself in the gilt-framed cheval mirror. The reflection showed her a tall, slim young woman in a cream, high-necked, long-sleeved blouse trimmed with lace collar and cuffs, a full-length deep blue serge skirt and a broad black belt encircling her small waist. Her heavy, corn-coloured hair had been pinned up by Rose into a chignon which suited her delicate features perfectly. Altogether, Elizabeth thought wonderingly, the picture she was looking at was an exact copy of an Edwardian young woman.

She had used those thirty minutes most profitably in another way, too. She had gathered a store of information from the talkative Rose about the other members of the Dinsdale family, so that she now felt facing all these strangers would be a little less of an ordeal.

She wasn't expecting to meet Edward's father, Samuel Dinsdale, at this time of day, as Rose had informed her that, 'The master's a very busy man, what with all his parliamentary duties an' all, people always wanting to tell him their problems…' with a sad shake of her head. He was, apparently, the local Member of Parliament.

She wondered which party he represented, but as she didn't expect somebody in Rose's position to understand what kind of politics the master of the house would support, she decided to wait until she could ask Edward later.

But she had learned the names and some titbits of information about all the other members of the family, so, as she followed Rose downstairs, she wondered what each one looked like.

The broad, curving, mahogany-balustraded staircase led into a square hallway with a polished wooden floor covered with a brightly patterned square of carpet in shades of red and blue. This seemed to be the centre of the house, for there were half a dozen doors set evenly around the three sides of the hall not taken up with the broader door with windows on either side, which was obviously the main door to the outside.

Rose stopped by a door on the right, hesitated a moment, looked back to ensure that Elizabeth was immediately behind her, and then tapped on the door.

A pleasantly modulated female voice called out, 'Come in.'

Rose patted her cap, opened the heavy door, and stepped back to allow Elizabeth to enter.

Elizabeth noticed that the room was light and spacious, but had no time to take in details. A middle-aged, dark-haired woman in a plum-coloured dress was moving towards her, smiling, her hands outstretched in welcome.

'Good morning, my dear, how good to see you looking so rested. Are you feeling better this morning?'

Elizabeth knew immediately, without any introduction, that this was Anne Dinsdale, Edward's mother. She was a tall, dignified woman and Elizabeth noted, as she took the proffered hands and smiled in return, answering the question with, 'Yes, thank you, I'm feeling very much better today,' that she had the same deep brown eyes as her son.

'My husband's mother, Mrs Helen Dinsdale.'

Elizabeth offered her hand to the little old lady in the black bombazine dress and stiff bonnet who was sitting in a high-backed, winged armchair in the corner of the room farthest from the window. But her hand was ignored. Instead she was treated to a sharp gaze from a pair of faded, yet still piercing eyes which looked her carefully up and down and seemed to be staring right through her.

Having scrutinised her thus closely, the old lady emitted a snorting sound which could easily have been contempt, then dropped her gaze and returned to the contemplation of her secret thoughts.

Elizabeth felt most uncomfortable. She had the strange feeling that the old lady had already forgotten her presence.

Anne Dinsdale smiled apologetically and spoke quietly to Elizabeth as they moved away into the room.

'Don't take any notice, my dear, she's old now and rather crotchety. Her hearing's very poor and this makes her feel isolated. Sit here,' she indicated an armchair near the window, 'and I'll introduce you to the rest of my family.'

She turned to two young people in the middle of the room. Elizabeth recognised from Rose's information the fifteen-year-old twins, Rupert and Marianne.

Rupert was leaning against the ornately carved marble mantelpiece in a brown knickerbocker suit with a white Eton collar. He was trying to seem nonchalant and manly, but succeeded only in appearing gauche and ill-at-ease. Seeing his mother's warning gaze, he awkwardly offered Elizabeth his hand and shook it, blushing scarlet. Then, with a muttered apology to his mother, he hurriedly left the room.

Marianne, on the other hand, could hardly keep still in her eagerness to meet this stranger, and she wasn't in the least quelled by her mother's reproving look. Long dark curls bobbing and those same deep brown eyes sparkling, she was bubbling with excitement as she grabbed Elizabeth's hand.

'I'm thrilled to meet you, Elizabeth. It's just like a mystery story, you being found by Edward by the lake and being brought back here, and nobody knowing you. And you not remembering who you are or anything. It's absolutely thrilling!'

She was still holding Elizabeth's hand, pumping it up and down fervently, and the older girl couldn't help laughing.

Marianne's mother, however, was not amused by her daughter's behaviour.

'Marianne, will you please stop prattling like a character from a cheap novelette and let go of Elizabeth's hand directly? This young lady is a visitor in our home and will be treated with the same good manners that I expect you to show to any other visitor. And you are setting a very bad example to the little ones.'

It was only then that Elizabeth noticed a little head peering round the chintz-covered sofa in the centre of the room.

'This is my granddaughter, Amy Dorothea.'

Anne Dinsdale took the little girl's hand and led her forward.

'She's not usually so shy,' she said. 'But I'm sure it won't be long before she gets used to you, and then you won't be able to stop her talking.'

Elizabeth was struck by the little girl's beauty. The delicate face seemed filled by two huge blue eyes, fringed by silky lashes. Her deep green dress was topped by a white starched pinafore and she wore green slippers to match her dress.

But it was her hair that made her such a contrast to the dark Dinsdales. The sunlight pouring through the long windows was striking vivid tones of glowing copper, flaming orange, and warm gold in the reddest hair Elizabeth had ever seen. She gasped in amazement as the small figure bobbed a half-curtsey and smiled at her winningly.

'She's so different to the rest of you,' she exclaimed.

'Yes,' replied Anne, looking down at her little granddaughter fondly. 'She's my daughter Helen's child, but there's hardly anything of her mother in her looks. She takes after her father. That's where her incredible red hair comes from. And she has a flaming temper to match!

'But where's her sister hiding? Wherever Amy is, Millicent is never far away, so she must be here somewhere…'

The little girl darted back behind the sofa and appeared again triumphantly, dragging an even smaller child behind her.

'Here's Millie, Grandmama,' Amy announced, her

red curls dancing in triumph.

The tiny tot tried to hide behind her bigger sister.

'Millie's very shy,' Amy told Elizabeth, much more confident now that she had her small sister to crow over. 'But she's only three and I'm nearly five.'

They were certainly chalk and cheese in appearance. Tiny Millie had the usual Dinsdale colouring – dark hair and dark eyes. Only the starched white pinafore matched her sister's: this one topped a pale pink dress sprinkled with deeper pink rosebuds.

The little girl pushed a comforting thumb between her pearly teeth and stared at Elizabeth solemnly.

'The girls are visiting me for a few months to allow their mother to rest,' Anne explained. 'She's expecting again, and her physician is concerned about her health. He's worried that she may have an early confinement if she doesn't rest, and that's difficult with these two lively little people around!'

She turned to Marianne.

'Where's Adam? I told him to be here to be introduced to our visitor.'

'You know what he's like, Mama, forgets everything the minute you've told him. I expect he's in the stables, helping Joe to feed and clean out the horses. Shall I fetch him?'

'No, thank you, Marianne. I don't want him running in here covered in dirt and smelling of horses. You'll be able to meet my youngest child later, Elizabeth. Oh, we keep calling you Elizabeth, but I understand from Mrs Lane that you're not certain it's your name...'

She broke off with a questioning look.

'I think it must be, Mrs Dinsdale. There was a notebook in my pocket with the name "Elizabeth Carter" inside, which sounds familiar to me. I feel happy to be called Elizabeth, but I can't remember anything about my home or family. It feels very strange to have no memory of my life before I came here, and very unsettling.'

'I am sure it must be most uncomfortable,' Anne agreed sympathetically. 'And we must begin trying to trace your family at once. Now let me see...'

She mused for a few moments.

'Now, there's a family named Carter who moved into the village only a few months ago. Although they are newcomers, I have met Emily Carter a few times socially, so I think, under the circumstances, it would be in order to invite her to tea. I remember meeting two sons, but I didn't think she had any daughters. Perhaps you're a niece or a cousin…?'

'I really don't know.' Elizabeth shrugged helplessly. 'The name means nothing to me.'

'Well, I'll send a note round to ask her to tea this afternoon,' Anne decided firmly. 'Now, my dear, you must be hungry after sleeping so long. Would you like some breakfast?'

'Yes, please,' Elizabeth replied gratefully. 'I feel very hungry now.'

'Come into the dining room and I will ask Henry to bring you a cooked breakfast and fresh coffee. When you've eaten, perhaps you would like to stroll in the grounds? Marianne will show you around.'

Chapter 9

Elizabeth's hunger was soon satisfied with a large plate of bacon, sausages, eggs, and tomatoes with three slices of hot, buttered toast, washed down by several cups of coffee, served by a solemn uniformed butler at the long polished table in the oak-panelled dining room.

Feeling full of energy (and food!), she was ready to explore the grounds of Highwood Hall with the effervescent Marianne.

'Can you really remember absolutely nothing about your life before you came here?' the younger girl asked as they walked across the lawn towards the rose arbour.

To be more correct, Elizabeth was walking: Marianne couldn't control her exuberance enough to be so sedate. She jigged and skipped more in keeping with the age of her red-headed niece than befitted a young lady of nearly sixteen. Her mother would have been shocked to see her, but to Marianne, out of sight meant out of mind, and she was too eager to learn more about this stranger to care whether her mother would approve of her behaviour.

'Absolutely nothing,' the older girl confirmed with a smile. Already she was beginning to like this bubbly girl with her bouncing brown curls and sparkling brown eyes, so like those of her elder brother.

There was no reason to pause in the rose gardens. It was too early in the year for there to be any blooms to admire, although the unseasonal sunshine had started the brown thorny twigs swelling into new growth.

But beyond the rose gardens was a large rockery, and its grey stone walls were ablaze with colour, blue and yellow, purple and snow-white, from the spring bulbs planted by old Ben Hardwicke, the gardener, the previous autumn and many more years before.

'How lovely,' Elizabeth exclaimed, and stooped to admire the flowers, appreciating the magical beauty of spring growth. Marianne was impatient to move on, but, as she crouched there, Elizabeth had a sudden flash of déjà vu. She knew with certainty that she had recently admired these flowers or some very like them in a similar setting.

She tried hard to remember in more detail, but the brief tantalising glimpse into her memory had already vanished.

'Come on, let's go to the stables.' Marianne tugged at her arm impatiently. She was so eager that Elizabeth gave in gracefully, took the younger girl's hand in hers, and together they ran, laughing, along the gravel path which led to the stables.

Elizabeth could hear the whinnying of horses and jingling of harness before they reached the stables.

The path curved round a barn wall, which muffled the sound of their approach.

As the girls rounded the bend and entered the stableyard, Elizabeth saw a couple standing at the far end. Their dark heads were close together, but, as the woman was several inches shorter, she was looking up at him. Even at that distance it was obvious that their relationship was an intimate one.

The couple were unaware of the girls' presence: they had eyes only for each other. At that moment the man leaned forward and kissed the upturned mouth.

'That's enough of the lovey-dovey stuff, you two,' Marianne called gaily as she rushed towards them. The pair swung round and Elizabeth saw that the man was Edward.

The young woman with him was Henrietta. Her identity was obvious to Elizabeth, not only because Rose had told her the couple planned to marry, but also because the description of Henrietta the maid had given her fitted this young woman exactly.

She was actually quite tall, appearing short only in relation to Edward's greater height. In fact, her height and slim build matched Elizabeth's.

She wasn't beautiful, her appraiser decided – rather, she would have described her as striking. With dark hair pinned neatly under a broad-brimmed hat tied on with a chiffon scarf, her upright stance giving her elegance, and her trim figure encased in a navy riding habit, she made an attractive picture. Then, as she was introduced to her, Elizabeth discovered Henrietta's best feature. She had the most unusual violet-blue eyes. She certainly wasn't a classic beauty, but those eyes made her unforgettable.

And she spoke so charmingly to Elizabeth. It wasn't surprising that Edward was in love with her, she thought. How could any man help falling in love with this delightful girl?

But what she found very difficult to understand was why she should feel so jealous of this young woman…

She didn't have long to savour this feeling, for round the corner of the stable block hurtled a small boy. He was laughing as he ran and calling out to someone behind him who was invisible to the group. He was so engrossed in his enjoyment of the joke that he didn't see them, and the next moment he ran straight into Elizabeth, winding her and knocking her off balance. If Marianne hadn't caught her arm, she would have fallen to the ground with the small boy.

'Adam, you stupid boy!'

Edward had pulled up the little boy and was shaking him in exasperation.

'Why don't you look where you're going? Running into a visitor like that, you might have hurt her!'

The child – whom Elizabeth could see now wasn't more than about six, and who was covered with mud – began crying, partly from fright and partly from pain. His knees had made hard contact with the unyielding concrete yard.

'Don't be too hard on him, Edward,' she said, smiling kindly at the sorry figure. 'He didn't mean any harm. He was just playing.'

'Go on, then, young Adam, get back to the house at once and clean yourself up,' his older brother admonished him. But he spoke more gently this time and Elizabeth could see his fondness for the little boy.

'And do stop rubbing your eyes, you're making yourself look worse than ever!'

She couldn't help but agree with Edward's comment as the woebegone child walked away. His face was smeared with tear-tracks through the dirt, and Elizabeth was sure she hadn't met young Adam at his best!

Chapter 10

The tea party that afternoon looked set to be a total disaster.

Emily Carter turned out to be a quiet, self-effacing woman with no conversation beyond monosyllables of agreement with whatever anyone else said. She seemed to hold no opinions of her own on any topic, and a great number of subjects were brought up by Anne Dinsdale, who became more desperate as the interminable afternoon dragged on.

The children, fidgety as always when expected to sit demurely through boring adult conversation, were more badly behaved than usual. This party seemed extra dull to them, and even the special small sponge cakes topped with pink, white, and yellow icing couldn't make it enjoyable enough for them to remember their manners.

When Adam – a much cleaner, tidier small boy than had been seen earlier in the day, but still just as lively – leaped to his feet in response to a provoking comment from cheeky Amy, and knocked the cakestand from the wheeled trolley in the centre of the sitting room, Anne Dinsdale could take no more.

'Go to the nursery at once, Adam,' she commanded sternly.

'But Amy said she was going to eat the last cake with the yellow icing,' the outraged child said indignantly. 'It's not fair, she's already had more than me, and she knows the yellow ones are my favourites.'

'That's quite enough, Adam. I command you to go to the nursery and stay there until I send for you. Neither of you will have the cake. I'm ashamed of you both.'

Her grandmother's voice was so unusually sharp that little Millie suddenly burst into noisy tears. Even Amy, who was grinning at Adam's discomfort, had enough grace to look abashed.

'I think you'd all better leave us,' Anne said, feeling very embarrassed in front of their guest. 'Marianne, please take the children to the nursery and explain to Nanny what's happened. I don't want to see any of them again until their suppertime.'

Rupert, thankful for the diversion, managed to slip out with the chastened group, leaving Anne, Elizabeth, Henrietta, and Edward with Emily Carter and the huddled figure in the high-backed armchair in the corner.

She was still dressed entirely in black with the stiff bonnet shading her face from the last rays of daylight which could penetrate so far into the room. As it was now nearly five o'clock, it was already twilight, but Helen Dinsdale was taking no chances. She sat with her chair turned away from the windows, and thus she also had her back to the assembled company. But that didn't prevent them hearing quite clearly her quavering voice as she complained about the children's behaviour.

'Disgusting,' she addressed the wall in front of her. 'In my day, children had to behave respectably at all times, but especially in front of visitors, if they were fortunate enough to meet any, that is. I wasn't allowed to join adults at tea until I was twelve, and I wouldn't have dared to speak. I had to sit perfectly still with my hands folded in my lap until I was offered a slice of bread and butter or a sandwich…'

The querulous voice fell to a low mutter, then rose again as the old lady flung her final words at the wall.

'Children should be seen but not heard?' There was a snorting sound. 'Hmph! In my view, children should not be seen or heard until they are old enough to behave in a proper manner!'

Elizabeth felt sorry for Anne, who was scarlet with embarrassment and trying to apologise to her guest.

'My dear Mrs Dinsdale, please don't worry a moment longer. I know just what young children can be like when you want them to be on their best behaviour – little devils seem to get inside them! And as for your mother-in-law…'

Emily Carter's voice dropped, and she leaned towards Anne in a conspiratorial manner.

'No one could be more unpleasant than my husband's mother. She never has a good word to say about anybody, not even her son. I thank God that she didn't want to come to us when she grew too old to live alone. Her daughter has that pleasure, and she looks quite worn out and flustered whenever we see her.'

She smiled and patted Anne's hand. Her smile was warm and lit up the rather plain, pale face so that it appeared quite attractive. She was transformed into a different person from the drab, monosyllabic, middle-aged woman who had been so difficult to entertain just a short time before.

'You're very kind,' Anne said gratefully. 'Many people wouldn't be so understanding. And please call me Anne, it's so much less formal now that we're friends.'

'To tell you the truth, Anne, I'm relieved to see that your family is so ordinary. Oh, I'm sorry, I didn't mean to sound rude. I simply meant that you're so normal... oh, dear, I'm making things worse...' She stopped in confusion, and it was her turn to blush with embarrassment.

Anne's melodious laugh rang out in the suddenly quiet room.

'Shall we start this party again?' she enquired.

'Yes, please,' her guest confirmed gratefully. 'I was so nervous when I arrived that I couldn't think of anything interesting to say. I thought you were all so much better bred than my family are, with your husband being the local Member of Parliament and owning so much land round here, that I was tongue-tied. When your children misbehaved and your mother-in-law criticised their upbringing, I realised that your family is just like mine.'

'Speaking of families reminds me why I invited you here at such short notice,' Anne said, smiling in recognition of the truth of Emily's words. 'I thought it best not to bring up the subject in front of the children. You know how young ones prattle, and we don't want odd rumours circulating in the village…'

She broke off as she noticed the other woman was looking rather alarmed.

'Oh, my dear, I've worried you. Let me put your mind at rest. Do you recognise this young woman?'

Anne indicated Elizabeth, who smiled hopefully at Emily Carter.

'No. I'm sorry, I don't. Should I know her?'

'Well, we hoped that you would. As she shares your surname, and your family hasn't lived in the village long, we thought she might be a distant relative we hadn't met.'

'We're quite a small family,' Emily said, shaking her head doubtfully. 'Just me and my husband and our two sons – except for the old dragon and my husband's sister's family, of course. But she does remind me of someone. I can't think who it is at the moment…'

Elizabeth was uncomfortably conscious of the gaze of four pairs of eyes. Then Henrietta said suddenly: 'I know who Elizabeth looks like – young Sarah Anstruther. You know, Marianne's friend at school. She doesn't see so much of her now that Sarah's had to leave to help out the family finances since Mr Anstruther had an accident at the factory, but don't you remember her?'

'Oh, yes, dear. Sarah's much younger, of course, about a year younger than Marianne. But she has the same fair hair and those unusual green eyes, I remember. I wondered when I first met you, Elizabeth, where I had seen such green eyes before. Perhaps you're related to the Anstruthers?'

'Elizabeth?' Edward was concerned as she didn't answer, but seemed to be standing rigidly, lost in thought. She suddenly shook her head as though to clear it.

'I'm sorry, Mrs Dinsdale, I really don't know. Perhaps if I were to meet them?'

'Dare I risk another tea party?' Anne Dinsdale said ruefully.

Emily Carter laughed.

'This afternoon has been a real pleasure, Anne. I'm delighted to have had had the opportunity to meet your charming family, and I hope I may return the invitation soon. I'm quite sure that my sons – James and Thomas – will enjoy meeting such pretty young ladies!

'And now, my dear, I really must leave. My menfolk will be home soon with enormous appetites, and they don't like having to wait for their dinner!'

Anne crossed to the mantelpiece and pulled the tasselled rope hanging beside it. A moment later, Henry, the butler, appeared after a discreet knock at the door, and Emily Carter rose to leave.

'I hope the mystery of your identity is unravelled soon, my dear,' she said kindly to Elizabeth, and the younger woman smiled and nodded in agreement.

And Anne Dinsdale felt, although the mystery had not yet been solved, that the afternoon hadn't been the disaster she had feared half an hour before.

*

Edward was still watching Elizabeth closely. Though she had responded pleasantly enough to Emily and Anne, she seemed distracted.

'You recognised the name of Anstruther, didn't you?' he asked her quietly. 'Why didn't you say so?'

'It was a shock,' she admitted. 'Just for a moment a flash of memory came back to me, but I didn't want to be questioned until I'd had time to think. You see, the shock was…' She hesitated. 'I think my maternal grandmother's name was Sarah Anstruther…'

'But that's great,' Edward said excitedly. 'Anstruther is a very unusual name, so this could mean that *this* Sarah Anstruther could be related to you – a cousin, perhaps? We should go to the village straight away and speak with her!'

'No, no, Edward, please don't rush me. I could be wrong, and I don't want everyone to get excited on my behalf and it doesn't come to anything.'

*

Elizabeth couldn't get the flash of memory out of her head. She tossed and turned in her bed that night, trying desperately to recall anything else connected with her grandmother and the Anstruther name. But she could recall no more.

She decided that she must meet Sarah Anstruther and see if she could move forward. At breakfast the next morning, she waited until she and Edward were in the dining room alone, then asked him if he would drive her into the village.

Edward was only too keen. 'Fetch your wrap when

you've finished eating and I'll ask Robert to get the trap ready and bring it round to the door. It won't take us long to reach the Anstruthers' house.'

Before long they were in the trap, with Edward handling the reins expertly as they headed towards the nearby village. As they reached the first houses, Elizabeth felt more and more nervous. Who would this young woman turn out to be? A relative she would recognise or no connection at all?

'This is the house,' said Edward as he pulled up the trap at the side of a small cottage and jumped down to help Elizabeth alight. As she did so a young woman appeared, throwing handfuls of corn to a few hens clucking in the small garden.

They stared at each other in amazement. Both had hair the colour of ripe corn and the most remarkable green eyes. The two girls could have been twins, or at least sisters, as she was a few years younger than Elizabeth.

As both were speechless, it was left to Edward to explain why they were there. Sarah recovered first and smiled at Elizabeth. 'Well,' she said, 'we may not know each other but I think we must be related in some way. Please come in and take a cup of tea with my family and let's see what we can find out.'

She turned to the cottage door, then blushed, embarrassed. 'This isn't the kind of house you're used to, sir, so I apologise for that.'

'Don't give me a thought, Sarah,' Edward reassured the young woman. 'If I know anything about the people who live in these cottages, their homes are spotless, and yours is the same. And I'm as keen as Elizabeth to find out who she is!'

Unfortunately, though, that wasn't to be. Edward was right about the little home being clean and the family was welcoming, but, much as they enjoyed their chat over a cup of tea, none of the Anstruther family was able to say with certainty if Elizabeth was one of them.

But at least she drove back to Highwood Hall knowing she had made a firm friend in the girl who was a younger image of her.

Chapter 11

Elizabeth spent the new few days learning to adjust to the strange new circumstances in which she had found herself.

She enjoyed spending time in the large, warm kitchen, full of laughing, bustling women producing appetising smells from freshly baked bread, puddings, and pies. With the exception of the stern Henry, who considered himself a cut above the other staff, and disapproved of Elizabeth spending time with them, all the household staff seemed to enjoy her company and were prepared to answer her many questions.

Ada, the plump, red-cheeked cook, took such a liking to this quiet young woman that she even gave Elizabeth one of her huge white aprons and allowed her to roll up her sleeves and help mix the flour and eggs for a batch of cheese scones after Elizabeth told her they were a speciality of hers. The jolly cook felt sorry for the young woman's dilemma and thought that letting Elizabeth mix the scones would not only give her something useful to do, but might also trigger other memories of her past life.

As the batch of scones, hot and floury, were taken triumphantly from the big range to admiring comments from the cook and kitchen maids, Elizabeth had another flash of déjà vu – but again, she couldn't remember more details.

The cheese scones were delicious. She had remembered the recipe so easily and the results were so successful that she knew she had often made them before – but where and for whom? She wished she could remember…

The nursery was another favourite place. Nanny welcomed her with a restrained manner the first time she visited. But Elizabeth quickly showed she had a talent for making up stories to fascinate little minds, and it wasn't long before the appearance of Elizabeth's head round the door of the nursery brought a smile of approval to the rather severe features of the angular Miss Black, and whoops of delight from Adam, Amy, and Millicent.

'Tell us another story, Elizabeth,' they chorused with excitement.

'Children, where are your manners?' Miss Black admonished them.

'Pleathe, Lithbeth,' little Millie begged shyly.

Elizabeth couldn't resist those large pleading brown eyes.

'Up you come, then,' she smiled, whisking the toddler high into the air until the little girl giggled happily. Then she would sit with Millicent on her knee and the older two pressed close beside her, and invent fantastic tales of dragons and hobgoblins, beautiful princesses and handsome princes.

Sometimes the princess would be lively, with flaming red hair and blue eyes. Sometimes she would be quiet and shy, with lustrous dark curls and brown eyes – but she would always be the most beautiful girl in the land.

Elizabeth would invent more and more complicated and improbable stories, and the girls' eyes would grow larger and rounder, their lips parted in great concentration, as the princesses became involved in ever more exciting and dangerous situations.

She kept a close eye on young Adam as she allowed her imagination to run riot, and just when she sensed his impatience was ready to explode with anticipation and frustration, the handsome hero with dark hair and eyes would come riding to the rescue on a milk-white pony. Adam's eyes would glitter brightly and he would explain excitedly: 'That's me! I'm rescuing the princess!'

'You're a wonder with those children, miss,' the nanny said with an admiring note in her usually sharp voice. 'When these three get together it usually means trouble and tears before very long. But since you've been here they've been quite different. I've never known them so easy to handle. Perhaps you have children of your own?' she asked with a questioning look at the wedding ring Elizabeth was wearing.

'Oh, no, I'm sure I haven't,' the younger woman replied decisively. 'I couldn't believe I would forget my children if I had any.

'It's odd, though, I don't feel married, although I

suppose I must be, because of this ring. But I've absolutely no idea what my husband is like. I can't remember anything about him, not even his name.'

*

Elizabeth also spent a lot of time in the beautiful grounds of the manor house, usually with Marianne chatting away nineteen to the dozen beside her. She enjoyed the vivacious teenager's company and frequently had to hide a smile at the younger girl's enthusiastic and ingenuous comments on everybody and everything.

But sometimes Marianne had to disappear indoors for a hated piano lesson or to mend a lace frill on a petticoat she had torn in a too-hasty change of clothing when she was keen to be off somewhere.

The household employed plenty of staff to deal with such chores – in fact, it was one of Rose's tasks to mend the torn seams and drooping hems and replace the missing buttons of the ladies' clothes – but Anne Dinsdale was fed up with the frequent repairs which her tomboy daughter's clothes required, and thought that insisting Marianne repaired her own torn garments might make her mend her ways.

She often felt she was fighting a losing battle against the headstrong girl, but she could be equally determined, and she had no intention of letting Marianne become a spoiled and selfish young woman who believed that others would take responsibility for her carelessness.

Fond of the young woman as she was, Elizabeth was sometimes glad that these duties called Marianne into the house. Then she could wander round the huge grounds alone, stopping where she chose and breathing in the soft spring air, relaxing in the early sunshine.

She was drawn over and over again to the colourful rockery beyond the rose garden. Standing there, admiring the variety of plants from the tiny deep blue grape hyacinths and miniature yellow trumpets of the rock daffodils to the stiffly arching stems of golden-flowered forsythia and the sweet perfume of the jasmine reminded her… of what? Where? She was sure that somewhere here lay the key to the mystery of her forgotten past…

Day after day she wandered slowly round the rockery, bending to admire a tiny delicate bloom or smell a perfumed flower… and every now and then a fleeting memory would enter her mind, only to vanish before her conscious mind could fasten clearly upon the image.

Elizabeth found the experience at times deeply disturbing, and was distressed and worried by her inability to recall anything of her past life. She also had the strangest sensations that she knew about events that had not yet happened. Perhaps she was psychic, with the ability to see into the future. And yet there were many days when, as she strolled slowly around the rock garden, she felt calm, contented and at peace…

Chapter 12

She was standing by the rockery, lost in her thoughts, early one sunny day when a clear voice behind her said: 'Good morning, Elizabeth. How are you this glorious morning?'

She whirled quickly, her thoughts in confusion. She had been miles away, trying to recapture a memory of her past, and Edward had come up behind her without attracting her attention until he spoke.

She blushed and dropped the gloves she had been carrying. Edward bent down at the same moment as Elizabeth to retrieve them and they almost collided as they straightened up.

'Steady!' Edward warned as he grabbed at her arm. 'How would you like to come riding with me around the estate? There's a lovely little mare that would just suit you, I'm sure.'

Elizabeth hesitated. It really was a perfect day for riding. But how would Henrietta feel about her disappearing with Edward? She started to broach the subject diffidently, but Edward interrupted.

'Henrietta won't object to us exercising the horses together. I'd ask her to join us, but I know she's gone into town in the trap today to do some shopping. So would you like to ride with me?'

He spoke with authority and Elizabeth knew she would enjoy the ride in his company, so she followed him to the stables without further comment.

The horses were soon saddled and they set off slowly down the road which led to the main gates of the estate. Edward watched Elizabeth carefully for the first few moments, but it soon became obvious to him that she was an experienced rider, handling her mount gently but firmly.

For her part, Elizabeth was enjoying the ride, although she was feeling a little unbalanced in her side saddle. When she had been in the stableyard, waiting for the groom to steady the little grey mare before she mounted, she had had a strong instinct to throw one leg over the horse just as Edward had done a moment before. She suppressed the urge immediately, because her next instinct had warned her that both men would have been shocked. And, looking at the shape of the pommel, Elizabeth realised her attempt would have been pretty painful! She laughed aloud and her horse whinnied in reply, as though she, too, were enjoying the joke.

The riders turned onto a right-hand track a hundred years before the main gates, and were soon out of sight of the house. The track sloped gently down through mature oak and elm trees, and Elizabeth concentrated on guiding the little mare as she picked her way delicately through the gnarled tree roots and bracken.

After a while, Edward reined in.

'Are you all right?' He turned in his saddle and looked back at her.

'Fine, thanks,' she answered him with a smile. 'I'm really enjoying myself. It's so peaceful here and the trees are lovely.'

'Right then. Follow me and keep your head down.'

And with that, Edward swung his big chestnut horse to the right, urged him forward, and, leaning low over his neck, pushed forward through the trees. It was dark and cool under the thick canopy of leaves, and Elizabeth enjoyed the moist, peaty smell and the quiet solitude. She and Edward might have been in a world of their own, and she felt more relaxed than she had done since this strange situation had begun.

Glimmers of sunlight began to dart through as the trees thinned out. Then, suddenly, Edward turned sharply to his left, and Elizabeth had to concentrate to make her horse turn as well. So it was that, as she lifted her head to see why Edward had turned, she had no inkling of what was in front of her.

She gasped, amazed. For there, laid out in all its splendour before her, was a shimmering river flowing through green banks lined with willows. The pasture sloped gently down towards it, and beyond, a tiny church spire peeped above high hedges. This idyllic picture was topped by a sky of cornflower blue without a wisp of cloud.

Edward had no need to ask Elizabeth if she liked what she saw. Her face gave him the answer.

'This is my favourite spot on the estate. I come

here as often as I can, especially when I need to think through a problem. Somehow whatever I'm worried about seems so much less important here. Would you like to sit and rest for a while?'

Edward leaped easily from his mount and moved to help Elizabeth. He was just in time, as she, forgetting the hampering effect of her long skirt, attempted to dismount just as lightly and almost tumbled to the ground.

'Careful!'

Elizabeth blushed in frustration and embarrassment as Edward's strong arms prevented her fall. The shock – or was it his closeness? – made her heart beat faster, and the concern in his dark eyes made her bite her lip and turn her head away in confusion.

'This is so beautiful! The light on the water and the gently sweeping movement of the willow trees. It's all so, so lovely…'

Her words trailed away as she realised how trite they sounded. But Edward took her hand, agreeing that words could not express such a scene adequately.

'Let's just sit quietly here and not worry about speaking for a while.'

They sat on the lush grass enjoying the scene, the only sounds the gentle rippling of the water and the contented munching of the horses. Elizabeth felt completely at peace. She didn't want to wonder or worry or rack her brains about who she was and how she had got there. This place – and this man for company – were all she wanted at this moment…

The time passed too quickly. The days were still

short and the warmth of the sunshine faded early.

'Would you like to ride with me again?' Edward asked her as they slowly rode back to the big house. One glance at her flushed face and clear sparkling eyes left him in no doubt as to the sincerity of her vigorous nod.

*

It wasn't long before the ride had become almost a daily habit. Each time she reached the gap in the trees and saw the shimmering cool water of the river, Elizabeth felt at peace – although she knew she was falling in love with this man who belonged to another woman.

Henrietta guessed, too, that their relationship was growing beyond mere friendship, but she felt helpless as Edward drifted further away from her each day. What could she do? They couldn't throw this stranger out when she didn't know who she was or where she belonged.

The final blow came when, one morning, unable to sleep, she wandered along the corridors of the house and saw Edward quietly creeping from Elizabeth's room. She stepped back into the shadows of the long curtains, feeling sick. She knew then, with certainty, she would never marry Edward…

Chapter 13

There was such excitement in the house. A dinner party like no other was planned for Easter Saturday, and everyone, from the senior staff to the youngest undermaid, had strict instructions that the evening must be perfect. No detail could be overlooked.

Cook was closeted in the morning room with the mistress of the house for much longer than usual. There would be five courses, starting with a clear soup, followed by sole in a cream sauce, roast beef with all the traditional trimmings – after all, the main guests could not have been more British! – a sharp lemon sorbet to clear the palate, and a Bakewell pudding with custard to finish. The meal would be completed with fine wines to complement each course.

'But who are these very important guests?' Elizabeth wanted to know.

'You must keep their names secret,' Edward told her, 'because if they get out there could be trouble. They are very influential. Mr Asquith, the prime minister, who was elected only two weeks ago, and his wife, who was formerly Margot Tennant, one of the famous Tennant sisters; Mr Churchill, made president of the board of trade just last week, and his companion, Clementine Hozier, who is expected shortly to become betrothed to him, are all invited. It should be a good evening, as all of these people are known to be excellent conversationalists.'

Elizabeth was shaken, but she tried to hide the fact. The names all sounded familiar to her – but from history books. Was she really going to sit down to dinner in such illustrious company?

The chosen evening was very cold. The fires had been stoked high, as snow was forecast, despite this being the middle of April.

Young Adam crept onto the landing to watch the guests arrive, peering through the banisters carefully so that he could see what went on below without being seen. As the great front door was opened, a burst of cold air flew in, and the butler hastened to close it again as soon as the guests were inside. As the visitors divested themselves of their many coats, scarves, and gloves, the butler caught the attention of a young housemaid who was scurrying across the hall.

'Here, girl, take these into the kitchen to ensure they're warm when the guests leave.'

'That's a good idea,' said the tall, distinguished man as he rubbed his hands together. 'I think the snow could arrive before the evening's out.'

Then Adam's eyes widened in amazement. The man had patted the housemaid's bottom as she took his scarf and gloves! He rushed into his sister Marianne's room, where she and Elizabeth were putting the finishing touches to their hair.

'That man has just touched Annie's...' He reddened as he realised he couldn't say the word without being in trouble.

'Annie's what?' his sister said irritably. Her little brother pointed to his own bottom without using the word.

'Oh, Adam, don't be ridiculous. A man in his position wouldn't do anything like that. Which man do you think you saw – the tall, distinguished one or the one with red hair?'

'The tall one!'

'That's the prime minister, you silly boy. Mr Asquith has his wife with him, she would never allow that.'

'She didn't see, no one saw. But Annie jumped and hurried away.'

Marianne shook her head and smiled. 'You were mistaken, Adam.' And she turned back to the mirror.

The dinner party seemed to go well. All the guests were on top form and pronounced all of Cook's carefully prepared dishes delicious.

If Samuel Dinsdale was surprised that Clementine Hozier glared at the prime minister a few times, he didn't show it. Perhaps it was the clumsiness of Mr Asquith, who dropped his napkin and then his fork, bending quickly to retrieve both before the footman could reach him, and leaning over Miss Hozier, his neighbour, as he did so, apparently staring fixedly at her décolletage, which caused the glare.

Elizabeth sat quietly, watching the performance,

noticing that, despite the other adults shifting uncomfortably and staring at their plates, Margot Asquith seemed completely oblivious to her husband's behaviour and kept the conversation flowing smoothly. Elizabeth was fascinated by this tall, slim, confident woman, dressed elegantly in a midnight blue shift with silver beading, sapphires sparkling in her ears and a matching pendant, although her features were too strong and mannish to enable her to be seen as beautiful or glamorous.

Fortunately, soon all three men became engrossed in the subject of the licensing bill which Mr Asquith hoped to shortly present to parliament.

'The government must tackle the problem of drunkenness and prevent young women from working in public houses,' he said. 'I feel so strongly about this that I am staking my political future and that of my party and my government on the successful passage of this bill through parliament.'

'But won't that mean many women losing their livelihoods?' asked Marianne. Her father glared at her as he raised his hand in warning. His daughter subsided into a fidgety silence as the men continued their conversation.

But when they turned to the subject of women's suffrage – on which Mr Asquith held very firm views – Marianne couldn't stop herself from another outburst.

'I cannot abide these strident young women who make scenes in public, screeching and carrying on like hoydens – most unseemly,' said Mr Asquith firmly. 'A well-brought-up young lady should act like one, and leave the subject of politics to her fathers, husbands, and brothers.'

'By what right do men have the say in how the country is governed, when half the population has no voice?' Marianne leaped to her feet in indignation.

'Marianne!' Both her parents tried to quieten their unruly daughter, but there was no stopping her.

'Women should be equal in politics, as they are in the sight of God…'

Her father was on his feet, frowning furiously, and her mother had paled at this embarrassing exchange. The guests were watching open-mouthed, even H.H. Asquith for once struck dumb at this unexpected onslaught.

Elizabeth acted swiftly.

'Come with me, Marianne, we need to freshen ourselves.' And she took the indignant girl so firmly by the sleeve that Marianne had to move with her. But the younger girl could not resist a parting shot as they reached the door. Wrenching herself from Elizabeth's grasp, she turned to the prime minister and spat out: 'I wouldn't vote for you even if I had the vote!'

The door closed behind them and there was a stunned silence for a moment before Samuel and Anne Dinsdale both tried to apologise for their daughter's behaviour.

'Don't give it a thought, my dears,' Clementine Hozier said soothingly. 'Your daughter was making a valid point. Women are just as important as men in their own way, and should play their part in the government of the country. I very much hope to do so during my lifetime, and I am sure many women agree with me.'

She looked to Margot Asquith for support. The older woman hesitated, unsure what to say which would be helpful, yet not appear critical of her husband. She looked from one to the other, her strong, rather masculine, jaw more pronounced than ever.

'It would be hypocritical of me to condemn Marianne's outspokenness, wouldn't it, Henry, my dear?' She smiled at her husband fondly. 'I have had a reputation for years around town for speaking my mind.

'However, since I married I have started believing that perhaps women are best suited to supporting their husbands quietly behind the scenes,' she said. 'They can be very supportive as wives and mothers, ensuring their husbands' lives run as smoothly as possible. I see that as my role, certainly while my children are young and need me so much.'

'How old are your children?' Anne Dinsdale had recovered her composure and now steered the conversation into easier channels.

'Elizabeth is eleven and Anthony five. And I can tell you that Elizabeth already has very determined ideas, so no doubt I will have to watch her as she gets older.'

Everyone laughed and the atmosphere relaxed as the guests helped the conversation flow smoothly again.

*

Back in her room, Elizabeth shook Marianne as the younger girl still argued vehemently.

'Be quiet and listen, Marianne. You won't get anywhere if you fight and argue with your elders. Believe me when I say that you will get what you want if you can just be patient. Women will fight for their rights – and some of them may be hurt or even die for their cause – but you WILL be able to vote in your lifetime, I am certain of that.'

Marianne had stopped wriggling and arguing, and she stared hard at Elizabeth.

'How can you be so sure? You're just saying that to make me be quiet, but I won't. I'm going back in that dining room to give that stuffy old man another piece of my mind. He's a dirty old man, too, staring at Miss Hozier's chest. And I believe Adam when he said he saw him pinching the housemaid's bottom. He's a hypocrite, wanting women to stay in their place and say nothing about his disgusting behaviour!'

'No, Marianne, this isn't the way to achieve what you want. All you will do is make your parents angry and encourage them to treat you as a spoiled child instead of an adult. To behave in that way at your first dinner party was thoughtless and rude, and now you are unlikely to be allowed to attend more adult occasions for some time. I suggest you apologise humbly and promise not to behave in that way again.'

Marianne looked mutinous and scowled.

'Oh, darling, don't sulk. I promise that you will be able to vote one day, and long before you're an old lady!' Elizabeth hugged the younger girl until a rather petulant smile appeared reluctantly.

'Now let's wash our faces and tidy our hair and then we can return to the dining room and you must make your peace with Mr Asquith as well as your parents. He may be behaving badly as the prime minister, but you don't have to stoop to his level. I know you can apologise prettily if you choose, and that's the only way you will be allowed to take part in adult gatherings.'

Marianne realised that Elizabeth was right. So she acted her part as a contrite young woman and hung her head in shame as she apologised for her outburst. By refusing to meet her parents' eyes they couldn't detect the gleam in hers and discover she wasn't contrite at all! But her apology was graciously accepted by the prime minister, who asked Samuel and Anne to forget all about it and put it down to youthful high spirits.

Chapter 14

'Please, Elizabeth, do come to the meeting with me,' Marianne pleaded for the umpteenth time. 'Mother won't let me go alone, but she's bound to agree if you say that you'll go with me and make sure I'm all right.'

'I don't know, Marianne, there could be a large crowd and that could mean trouble. People have such strong feelings about the suffragettes.' Elizabeth was worried.

'But it's such an important day,' urged Marianne. 'A day especially for women and their interests has never happened before. We would be making history. Please say you'll go with me.'

Elizabeth relented. 'Well, it would be interesting,' she admitted. 'But you must have your mother's permission. And promise me you'll stay close by me and be ready to leave at once if the crowd gets out of hand.'

Anne Dinsdale was reluctant to allow Marianne to go to the meeting, but, reassured by the knowledge that Elizabeth would watch out for her young daughter, she gave her consent.

Sunday, June 21st dawned bright and sunny, and, as they set off in the trap for London, Marianne couldn't contain her excitement. She leaned towards Elizabeth conspiratorially and spoke quietly so that Robert wouldn't hear her.

'Look, Elizabeth, I have ribbons for us both.' She held out two streamers of white, green, and purple ribbon, dropping one in Elizabeth's lap and tying the other over the white ribbon in her own hair.

'Why have you brought these?' asked Elizabeth.

'These are the colours of the women's movement and everyone who attends the rally has been asked to wear them for the first time to show support and solidarity for the cause. The purple stands for dignity, the white for purity, and the green for hope. Tie yours over your plain ribbon, then you can remove it when we leave.'

Elizabeth was stunned when they reached Hyde Park. Hundreds of thousands of people had turned up to celebrate the cause. For weeks beforehand squads of women on bicycles had toured London, plastering walls with posters and scattering leaflets in the streets, ensuring that everyone who was sympathetic to the cause of universal suffrage would know about the rally.

Thousands of women from all over England were drawn into the capital. In brilliant sunshine, charabancs brought them in, and many had marched miles behind brightly embroidered banners.

Speakers were on platforms above sections of the

crowd, and the greatest support was being given to Emmeline Pankhurst and her daughters, Sylvia and Christabel, who all gave impassioned speeches.

A young woman next to them turned excitedly to Elizabeth. 'Isn't this thrilling? So many people on our side, the government must take notice of us now!'

The speaker was a woman probably in her mid-thirties, Elizabeth judged. Slim, she was dressed in black, but the drab effect was enlivened not only by the purple, white, and green sash bearing the slogan 'Votes for Women' across her chest, but by the bright red curls flaring out around the black hat perched on her head. She was also wearing an armband bearing the word 'steward'. But her most noticeable attribute, to Elizabeth, anyway, were her bright green eyes, so like her own, alight with passion and excitement.

The speaker held out her hand.

'I'm Emily Davison. I'm a teacher at the moment, but I'm planning to give that up soon to work full-time for the cause. There's nothing as important as giving women the vote. We have been downtrodden for so long. And you?'

She shook Elizabeth's hand with fervour.

'I'm Elizabeth Carter. I believe that men and women are equal and I am sure that one day all women will have the right to vote.' She could speak with conviction because somehow she knew what she said was true.

'I must go and make my speech now,' said Emily. 'But please stay here and listen to me so that I can ask you what you think of it afterwards.' And the slim figure slipped through the crowd towards the speakers' platform.

Elizabeth listened with interest to Emily's speech. It was impassioned and fervent, and the crowd yelled and cheered with admiration.

Elizabeth tried hard to think why Emily Davison's name was familiar. So were the names of Emmeline Pankhurst and her daughters. But she was sure she had never met any of them before. Only the names – not the people – seemed known to her.

The effort of trying to remember and the shouts and cheers from the sea of white, green, and purple started to make Elizabeth's head ache. She wanted to tell Emily how good her speech was, but the teacher had been swept up in a sea of excited people. After several hours at the meeting she was feeling dizzy and nauseous.

'Marianne, I think we must leave now,' she said. 'Robert said he would arrive with the horse and trap at 5pm and it's nearly that, so let's make our way to the exit.' She started off determinedly, a chattering, excited Marianne dancing along beside her.

She was glad to see Robert patiently waiting for them and subsided gratefully into the trap, still feeling a little sick and pleased to be able to rest. As they left the crowd and London behind them and travelled into the country, she began to feel better.

As they neared 'home', however, a horrible premonition came over her. She knew that something was wrong, she could feel it without understanding what it was.

The trap swung into the long drive that led to the house, and the unpleasant feeling grew stronger. The smell of smoke hung in the air, and the horse whinnied and tossed his head as Robert tried to calm him.

'Now, boy, easy, easy.' And then they saw it. Flames were pouring from the windows of the house, licking round the frames and crackling in the rooms beyond. The sound of glass breaking added to the horror.

Robert slewed the trap to a halt, intent on rushing into the inferno, but the horse was too terrified to stand still. 'Marianne, can you take the trap round to the stables?' he asked her, knowing how good she was with all the horses. 'I must see if there's anyone inside the house.'

'I'm coming with you!' Elizabeth yelled above the noise.

'No, miss, you mustn't…' But he didn't finish his sentence, because Elizabeth was already running towards the burning house.

She had never been in a house fire before, and the heat and smoke nearly knocked her off her feet. Coughing and spluttering, she thought she would choke, and it took her several minutes to get her bearings.

She didn't know where to begin, but Robert realised that the drawing room would have been the most likely place for many of the family to have been at that time of day. Flinging open the heavy drawing room door, he was met by a wall of flame. It was impossible to see anything except the flames curling up the heavy curtains. He pulled the door closed and turned to Elizabeth.

'There are some horse blankets in the stables. I'll soak them in water and we can put them over our heads. Wait here. Try calling their names…'

He dashed off and Elizabeth stood in the smoke-filled hallway, calling out the names of the family, one after the other. She could hear no answering voices and she was undecided about which way to move.

Then an ominous crack above her head made her look upwards. A rafter from the vaulted ceiling had burned partway through. Before she could move aside, the damaged rafter fell, striking her head, and she slumped unconscious to the floor.

She was unaware that a strong pair of arms was half-lifting, half-pulling her through the front door. She didn't know that burning debris was raining down on her and her rescuer. He couldn't raise his arms to shield his face because of Elizabeth's weight. He only knew he had to drag her to safety. Once he had done that he, too, slumped unconscious from the effort and pain of his burns…

Chapter 15

1980

'I'm so worried about her,' Ben told his parents-in-law anxiously. 'I can't seem to get through to her, no matter what I try. I'm at my wits' end.'

The three of them stood at the living room window, watching Elizabeth mooching round the garden, apparently looking at nothing, lost in her thoughts. Now and again she would stop, peer closely at a flower or shrub, then wander on again.

'Have you talked to the doctor?' asked Maria. 'Yes, and he told me to give her time, not to chivvy her, because none of us knows what she's been through. He knew that she'd had a nasty bang on the head which didn't seem to have affected her physically, but may well have caused her to lose her memory.'

'She still can't tell you what happened to her?' queried John.

'I'm not sure if she can't, or she won't. You know

how stubborn she can be when she puts her mind to it. I don't want to be unkind, but I'm so worried and if I could just get through to her…' Ben's voice tailed away into a smothered sob, and Maria touched his arm in sympathy.

'We understand because we feel the same way,' she said. 'We keep trying to talk to her about things she used to show an interest in, but the only spark I've managed to arouse so far was with a book about the suffragettes.'

'That's strange,' said Ben. 'She has dreams about those women, too. The other night she suddenly screamed and when I took her in my arms she was sobbing bitterly. She told me that a young woman had thrown herself in front of the king's horse and she was too far away to prevent it happening. She talked about this girl as though she knew her!'

'That was Emily Davison,' said Maria. 'That story is in the book she was reading, and it is true. But it happened so long ago, in 1913, I think. She has such an imagination that I don't think she can always distinguish between what she reads and real life.'

Each night that dream filled Elizabeth's head. It was so vivid.

The press of people, the excitement, the noise, was incredible. The sound of thundering hooves as the horses swept round the curve was caught up in the shouting and the excited waving of hands and scarves.

Then she saw Emily. A still, quiet figure all in black, strangely at odds with the screaming exuberant crowd.

'Emily!' Her voice was lost in the sea of noise and movement. She pushed forward urgently, but the massed people were in no mood for someone to take their place against the rails and steal a better view of the race.

Suddenly the figure in black ducked under the guard rail and stepped in front of one of the horses.

'The king's horse!' came a shrill cry, then instantly, as the figure crumpled to the ground, the massive noise died away. Only the galloping hooves, swept along by their own momentum, could be heard in the eerie silence.

Something fluttered up from the hand of the crumpled woman, floated above the heads of the staring crowd towards the horrified Elizabeth. She stretched up and caught it. It was a scrap of green, white and purple ribbon…

And Elizabeth awoke in a pool of sweat, thrashing around and sobbing, 'Emily, poor Emily,' until Ben's strong arms around her, holding her firmly, soothed her back to sleep.

*

'Elizabeth,' said her mother, 'I've found this box of old photographs from the past. Would you like to look through it and see if there's anything to interest you?'

Reluctantly, Elizabeth took the box and sat down by the window. She turned over the first photos in a desultory fashion, glancing at them without interest. But soon she became engrossed in the grainy snapshots, trying to recognise family members and friends from the past.

Then she picked up a picture of a young woman,

and her heart beat faster. Smiling back at her was a likeness of herself – and across her chest was a ribbon stating 'Votes for women'.

'Sarah Anstruther!'

Her mother looked up from her sewing across the room, startled. 'What did you say, dear?'

'This picture is of Sarah Anstruther,' Elizabeth said excitedly. 'I know, because I've met her.'

Her mother came over to the window and took the photograph.

'Yes, dear, that is Sarah Anstruther. But you couldn't have met her. She was my mother – your grandmother – and tragically she died as a young woman. She was closely involved with the suffragettes, and the treatment they received ruined the health of many young women. She died when I was only a child, sadly just before universal suffrage was introduced in 1928. So she never managed to vote because she didn't own property.

'I expect she seems familiar because you are so much like her. As you grew up I was thrilled by how much you resembled the mother I had lost too soon. Not only do you look so much like her, but your passionate interest in the suffragettes and their cause is so much like her, too. I think she was disappointed that I was too young to be interested, but she would have been thrilled to have known that you shared her passion.'

She turned away, but Elizabeth had caught the glistening of tears in her eyes and put her arms around her mother. 'I'm sorry, Mum, I didn't mean to upset you. I was so sure I had met her that I thought I might be remembering something. But obviously I'm mistaken. And you're right, I do look just like her.'

Maria rooted about in the box and picked out a handful of photos.

'Here's Sarah on her wedding day, with your grandfather.'

This picture was more formal, showing a young woman with her hair pinned up, a huge bouquet of lilies and greenery.

'And this is me as a baby with her.' A proudly smiling young woman with a bundle in her arms.

'And this is one of her as a young girl, about fifteen, I think.'

But Elizabeth didn't need to see this faded sepia photograph. She had a full-colour picture in her mind of a laughing girl in a print dress topped by a starched white pinafore, her corn-coloured hair waving in the breeze, her bright green eyes sparkling as she ushered her in through the wooden door of a little cottage…

Chapter 16

'Would you like to go out somewhere?' Ben asked her gently at breakfast one morning. Elizabeth was staring at the table and didn't answer. He touched her arm and she jumped in alarm.

'Sorry, darling, I didn't mean to startle you. I just asked you if you would like to go out somewhere, to make a change from these four walls.'

Elizabeth pondered. 'Yes,' she said suddenly. 'I would like to go for a walk on my own.'

'No, darling, that's not a good idea…' Ben stopped as the familiar mutinous look appeared on Elizabeth's face.

'I meant it would be lovely if we went out together,' he went on hastily. 'I have missed you and time together would be great. Where would you like to go? The weather's warm enough for us to take a picnic lunch and make a day of it.'

'Highwood Hall,' replied Elizabeth. 'The grounds are lovely and there's a river and willow trees and a pond. I'd like to go there.'

Ben looked at her in surprise. 'Are you sure you mean Highwood Hall? That's been derelict for years, and the grounds are very overgrown. I'm not even sure if it's open to the public now, as it's considered unsafe.'

It was Elizabeth's turn to look surprised. 'Of course it's not. You must be thinking of somewhere else. Well, if we can't go there, we might as well stay here.' And she got up from the table with an air of finality.

Ben hastened to put his arms round her. 'I must have got it wrong,' he said soothingly. 'Obviously I'm thinking of somewhere else. Why don't you make some sandwiches while I pack the car with a blanket and other bits and pieces for the picnic?'

Out of earshot of Elizabeth in the kitchen, Ben made a quick call to her parents.

'Elizabeth has agreed to go out with me for a day in the countryside with a picnic,' he told John. 'I thought you would like to know that she is adamant about visiting Highwood Hall and won't go anywhere else.'

'Highwood Hall? But that burned down years ago and has been neglected for decades,' said John. 'Why does she want to go there?'

'Goodness knows,' replied Ben. 'I thought I must have muddled it up with a place of a similar name. Oh well, at least she's showing interest in going out, which is a start. I'll let you know how we get on.'

They were soon in the car and heading south into the countryside. Highwood Hall lay about five miles away, well within walking distance if Elizabeth had been fit and well, but Ben was taking no chances. He wanted to be able to drive away if he felt that was needed.

As they neared the wrought-iron gates, Elizabeth became agitated. Tall weeds were growing through the metal, and a tree had fallen against one gate at a drunken angle, so that it had fallen outwards, listing on its lower hinge. Hanging sideways from the top corner was a sign stating, 'Danger, unsafe building. Keep out.'

'This is all wrong,' she muttered, shaking her head. 'They would never allow this to happen.'

'Shall I drive on?' Ben asked her hopefully.

'No,' said Elizabeth vehemently. 'Drive up to the house.'

'I can't, Elizabeth. The drive is too overgrown.'

'Then we'll walk. I know it's not far.'

And with that, she was out of the car, had slipped through the gap in the gates, and was walking briskly up the drive. By the time Ben had found a safe spot off the side of the road in which to park the car, Elizabeth was out of sight.

'Wait for me, Elizabeth!' Ben might as well not have bothered to call after her, as she had no intention of waiting for him. He hurried as fast as the clinging weeds and nettles would allow, and finally saw the burnt-out ruin of the house ahead of him. The façade was blackened and forlorn, spaces where the windows had once been looking like empty eyes, and piles of stones clustered here and there with drifts of rosebay willowherb and ox-eye daisies softening the otherwise bleak aspect.

In front of this ruin stood Elizabeth, rigid and still. As he came up to her she turned an anguished face to him. Tears were streaming down her cheeks.

'I didn't think it really happened,' she sobbed. 'I thought it was just one of my nightmares. Did they all die?'

He held her tightly.

'Who?' he asked her gently. But she was crying too hard to answer him.

Chapter 17

Ben's patience was wearing thin. He kept trying to make allowances for Elizabeth's 'illness', but damn it all, they were married! She had every excuse in the book for not making love.

'I've a headache, I'm sorry, I'm too tired, perhaps tomorrow…'

He was worried, then alarmed. She just couldn't seem to recover and was becoming more and more withdrawn from him every day. She seemed to be living almost entirely in an imaginary world, a world of her own, and it frightened him.

Her odd behaviour was affecting him, too. He was jumpy, he couldn't concentrate properly on his work, and he wasn't sleeping well. Waking each morning with a leaden head and dull eyes, he would plod wearily off to the office, and he knew his anxiety about Elizabeth was affecting his work. Several times he had made elementary errors and had been sharply reprimanded. What was he to do? Things couldn't go on like this.

Then one night, when yet again he couldn't sleep, but lay tossing and turning next to a still, silent Elizabeth, he slipped out of bed to go to the bathroom. Then he went downstairs to the kitchen and poured himself a glass of cold milk from the fridge. He stood for a few moments, his head pressed to the cool glass of the kitchen window, staring out at the still night. The moon was bright and the fir trees in the garden stood out in sharp-etched relief against the clear sky. Gradually he quietened and felt more relaxed and at peace. He rinsed the glass under the tap, crept back upstairs and quietly entered the bedroom.

Ben looked down at the still-sleeping body of his wife. The moonlight was shining through a chink in the curtains, catching her tousled hair and making her curls glint. It clearly showed her face, her moist lips parted, her breathing even and shallow. One arm was flung across his pillow, palm up, her fingers curled gently in on themselves. Her cheeks were flushed and her eyelids were fluttering rapidly.

It was a warm night and, moving in her sleep, Elizabeth had pushed back the blankets so that only the sheet covered her body. Her thin nightdress had slipped so that the pinkish-brown nipple of one breast peeped coyly above the sheet, the downy swell of its owning breast highlighted in the shaft of light.

Ben stepped forward and lifted the sheet. Elizabeth lay sprawled on her back, her hidden arm now revealed to be across her stomach. Her thighs were parted and her fingers were entwined in the curls which glistened moistly in the moonlight.

Ben was suddenly filled with desire. Gently, tenderly, so that he wouldn't wake her, he began caressing her. He stroked the exposed breast with a gentle circular movement, round and round, over the globe, teasing the nipple, which now stood out proudly from the soft, warm flesh. Bending, he took it carefully between his lips, rolling his tongue round it, drawing it out, while Elizabeth writhed and moaned, moving her fingers against her now-wet mound. Ben moved his hand to join hers, sliding one finger gently between her thighs, increasing the pressure as she pushed her hips up to meet his exploring finger.

Gingerly Ben lifted his body over hers and let himself down gently onto his elbows so that his weight didn't wake her. If he alarmed her who knew how long it might take her to get over it? But there was no stopping her now: he had never known her to be so urgent, so responsive.

As he slipped inside her, Elizabeth's arms encircled him and they moved together. Faster and faster he thrusted. He could feel her passion rising and couldn't hold back. As he burst deep inside her he felt her climax shuddering in time with his, and felt at last that she had returned to him. He sobbed with joy.

Then she shouted: 'Oh, oh, Edward!'

Chapter 18

Ben was devastated. Was his beloved Elizabeth in love with another man? Had she met and slept with a stranger during those weeks she had been away from him?

He didn't know who to turn to. Her parents were hardly the right people to discuss this situation with. Finally, he decided to visit the family doctor. He was a straight-talking man, a doctor of the old school, who had known both the young people from their births and perhaps he could help Ben with this dilemma.

Doctor Brown listened carefully to Ben's halting explanation. When he reached the end, telling him how Elizabeth had called out another man's name as they climaxed, Ben's voice broke on a sob.

'Now, Ben, take it easy,' the doctor said briskly. 'What happened is upsetting, but you mustn't take it to heart. We still don't know what Elizabeth went through in those weeks away, but it could be that she was simply dreaming. Dreams are a wonderful way of getting issues out of our systems, and, as you say she didn't wake when you made love to her, she must have been sleeping very deeply. She probably doesn't know what she said.'

'But how are we to rebuild our relationship when there's such a gulf between us?' the distraught Ben asked.

'I suggest you try for a baby,' Doctor Brown answered soothingly. 'There's nothing better to keep a young woman occupied. Having a child to look after and care for will bring Elizabeth out of her reverie and firmly into the place she belongs. She won't have the time or the inclination to dream that she is somewhere else or in a different time. It's possible that you may have already achieved this…'

And the doctor was right in his supposition. Only a few weeks later Elizabeth missed a period, and the next month a second one. Doctor Brown was delighted to confirm that she was, indeed, expecting a baby, and patted her arm paternally as he said: 'Now, my dear, you have a busy time ahead of you and you must concentrate on keeping yourself fit and happy so that the little one will arrive well and you can take on your new role without worries.'

As her pregnancy progressed, Elizabeth seemed to have taken the doctor's words to heart, as she blossomed physically and mentally. Her scans showed a rapidly developing foetus – so much so that she surprised the nurse at her five-month check-up by presenting with a bump more usually pronounced than for such a term.

'Perhaps your dates are wrong…?' the young nurse asked her. Elizabeth just smiled and shook her head in the dreamy fashion everyone was becoming used to.

A month before her due date, Elizabeth went into labour. Ben rushed her to the local hospital, where, after only three hours, she gave birth to a healthy, full-weight son. As she happily cuddled him to her, Ben was surprised to see that he had dark curly hair and dark brown eyes, colouring quite unlike his own or Elizabeth's.

'He doesn't look like either of us,' Ben commented to Elizabeth in bewilderment.

'That's not unusual at birth,' the doctor soothed him. 'In a few days or weeks his colouring may change and you will see a resemblance to one of you or another immediate member of the family. Have you decided upon a name for him yet?'

'I thought we might call him after me or perhaps your father or mine,' suggested Ben. But Elizabeth, staring devotedly down at her baby son, didn't answer him. Then she crooned softly, 'Edward Oscar.'

'What was that, Elizabeth?' Ben bent close to her to catch her words.

'Edward Oscar, that seems to suit him.'

'But no one in our families has either of those names. Where did they come from?'

'Does it matter?' said Elizabeth sharply. 'I like those names and they feel right for my baby.'

'Our baby,' Ben corrected her. 'Well, if you really like them that much, I expect I can get used to them. But couldn't we add either Ben or John after me or your father?'

'If you like,' replied Elizabeth. And with that she

went back to cooing at her little boy.

*

'Edward Oscar!' Elizabeth's father said in disbelief. 'Where on earth did she get such fancy names? They're far too posh for the likes of us! No one in this family has ever been named in such a highfalutin fashion. What's wrong with Ben or John or even Tom after your father? Or perhaps another good, solid Biblical name…'

'She won't tell me where she found these names or why she's so set on using them,' said Ben. 'But you know what Elizabeth's like once she's made up her mind. And I don't want to upset her after all she's been through, especially as she's showing such an interest in the baby. I'm getting used to these names, although I would like her to accept either Ben or John as well, so that it feels more as though the baby belongs to both of us.'

'That's a good compromise.' John Carter nodded approvingly. 'Then he can be our little Ben or John, even if Elizabeth wants to call him Edward. Perhaps we can get her to drop the Oscar in favour of one of those names. The only Oscar I've ever heard of was Oscar Wilde, and I don't think we want any connotation of that sort, thank you very much!'

Chapter 19

'Are you sure it's wise to go out so soon?' Ben watched his wife anxiously as she buttoned her coat and tidied her hair in front of the hall mirror.

'Ben, I need some fresh air and so does Edward. I've had lots of rest in the last three weeks, and the doctors wouldn't have let us come home if they hadn't been sure we were both fine. Please stop worrying. I won't stay out long, but I want to take Edward to the church to offer a prayer of thanks for his safe delivery.'

Ben hugged Elizabeth and planted a kiss on her forehead.

'Okay, you win. I know it's no use arguing with you when you've made up your mind. But keep on the move, won't you? Although it's brighter today, there's still quite a cold wind, and I'd hate either of you to catch a chill!'

Elizabeth pulled a blue woollen hat firmly down over her ears, wound a matching fringed scarf round her neck, and picked up her gloves.

'There, is that better? I won't catch cold now. I'll be warm as toast!'

Edward was already asleep, tucked firmly in the blankets in his pram, his blue knitted bonnet and one white-mittened tiny fist peeping above the coverlet.

Ben watched Elizabeth until she was out of sight, then picked up the phone to call Maria – *Just in case*, he thought. Maria and John lived closer to the church and he knew she wouldn't mind looking out for Elizabeth.

Elizabeth pushed the pram proudly along the street towards St Benedict's. She had been brought up to attend the church regularly with her parents, and she and Ben had been married there. She didn't mind the walk of a mile or so. The people were so friendly, and she was looking forward to taking Edward with her. The vicar welcomed children, no matter how young, and she was sure he would be delighted to arrange the baby's baptism.

Today, she'd be even more glad to reach the church. Ben had been right – the wind was cold – and she walked briskly, barely glancing at the front gardens of the houses she passed, not stopping as she usually did to admire a fine shrub or border. She did notice, however, that there was still an odd patch of snow here and there which the wintry rays of sun hadn't reached.

As she turned thankfully under the lychgate at the entrance to the churchyard, and started pushing the pram along the stone-flagged path between the gravestones, she caught a snatch of organ music and realised that she wouldn't have the church to herself.

Still, if it was Mr Johnson practising for next Sunday's services, he wouldn't mind if she wandered round the church, running her fingers over the beautiful carved wooden choirstalls and reading the marble tablets set high in the walls. She liked to sit quietly in her favourite pew, imagining what the people commemorated in those tablets looked like and the kind of lives they led. What must it have been like to have lived in those long-ago days?

Ben teased her about what he called her 'romantic fancies', but Elizabeth hoped that Edward, as he grew up, would share her passion for the past. And, of course, her religious beliefs. If she set the foundations for her son this early, well, who knew…?

As she pushed open the heavy dark oak door and manoeuvred the pram, with some difficulty, down the broad stone step just inside, the organ music swelled. Mr Johnson – who had taken over as organist when his father died – was in fine form today.

She parked the pram at the back of the church and slipped into the last pew to pray.

After a few minutes, she rose, checked to see that the baby was still sleeping soundly, then made her way to the side chapel. There, on the white marble tablet next to the memorial window, were listed the members of the Dinsdale family who had lost their lives in a fire which had destroyed their home in June 1908.

Helen, widow of Edward Samuel, aged eighty-four; her son, Samuel, aged fifty-eight, and his wife, Anne, forty-five; their children… All the names were so familiar.

'Are you connected to the Dinsdale family?'

The soft voice made Elizabeth start. She had been so deep in concentration that she hadn't heard anyone enter the church, and she swung round sharply.

'I'm so sorry, my dear. I didn't mean to startle you.'

Elizabeth turned to see an elderly lady stooped over a silver-topped cane. Despite her great age – Elizabeth judged her to be at least ninety – she was elegantly dressed in a full-length navy blue coat of a style more reminiscent of the Edwardian age, with a small matching hat on her silver hair. But her eyes were those of a much younger woman. Elizabeth had only once seen such startlingly vivid violet-blue eyes, and their owner had been much younger...

'Henrietta... Hetty!'

'Forgive me, my dear, I've upset you. Your face is familiar, but I'm sorry I can't place you at the moment. My eyes are not what they were, my sight has nearly gone.'

The musical voice tailed off questioningly.

'Hetty, it's me, Elizabeth. Tell me what happened to Edward... did he die in the fire?'

'Elizabeth? I don't understand.' The stooped figure became agitated and she reached out to grab Elizabeth's coat. Immediately a woman in nurse's uniform appeared from the shadows.

'Please, miss, don't say any more. Miss Kerbridge becomes upset easily and her memories are those from long ago, not recent events. She lives so much in the past now that I bring her here often so that she can see the tablet and remember the family she lost. They mean more to her than anyone of today. Are you related?'

'No, but I am very interested in local history and have researched the family in so much detail that I feel I knew them intimately. I wondered if anyone survived that terrible fire and it seems that Miss Kerbridge did. But did Edward Dinsdale? They were planning to be married, and it seems she remained single?'

'Elizabeth, always Elizabeth. He wouldn't look at me after she went...' The old lady was sitting in the first pew now, her shoulders hunched, and the nurse patted her hand consolingly.

'This isn't the Elizabeth you knew so many years ago. This is a young woman with a baby. Don't get upset, Miss Kerbridge. She has the same name, that's all.'

She turned to Elizabeth and added quietly: 'Mr Dinsdale and Miss Kerbridge were, apparently, brought up together, but it seems that, despite his family expecting the two of them to marry, he met and fell in love with a young woman who turned up out of the blue. He saved her from the fire but she vanished afterwards and was never found. He was heartbroken, and, though they remained close friends, he couldn't marry Henrietta.

'Edward Dinsdale died twenty years ago, but Miss Kerbridge's memory isn't what it once was. As she's grown older she has started to live more and more in the past, and now, at ninety, she believes he is still alive and waiting for her around each corner. If you're interested in the family history, have a look at Mr Dinsdale's grave. It's the one with the tall white marble headstone on the left of the main path as you go towards the gate. You can't miss it and you'll find it interesting.'

'I must get home soon, my husband will be worrying about me being out for so long in the cold with the baby.'

'Ah, yes, of course,' said the nurse. She spoke more loudly. 'The young lady is leaving now, Miss Kerbridge.'

The elderly figure straightened immediately, held out her hand and smiled.

'How rude of me, I forgot to introduce myself. Henrietta Kerbridge… although that's such a mouthful, my friends usually call me Hetty. Have we met before? I cannot see very well now and faces aren't always clear.'

The nurse gave a warning shake of her head, so Elizabeth said nothing, but took the proffered hand and squeezed it gently.

Hetty Kerbridge hesitated, as though trying to recall something, then her body slumped again and the silver head drooped.

With difficulty, Elizabeth manoeuvred the pram up the step into the porch. As she struggled, the pram bounced and Edward woke and started to cry. His mother made soothing noises, but the indignant baby refused to respond. Walking briskly down the path made no difference; the crying grew louder.

'Okay, out you come, just for a couple of minutes.'

Rocking Edward in her arms quietened the crying to sobs. She spotted the Dinsdale grave just a few yards away from the main path, and held Edward tightly in her arms as she looked down at the marble headstone.

'Here lies Edward Oscar Dinsdale, born October 12th, 1883, died January 1st, 1960. A brave man who risked his life trying to save his family from a fire. He failed, yet saved the life of a stranger, Elizabeth Carter.'

Suddenly she felt completely at peace. The baby had stopped crying and seemed to be staring into the distance.

The wind caught at Elizabeth, but she didn't notice. A few dry leaves rustled and swirled in a giddy dance on the gravel path nearby.

Suddenly, she came to – it was cold and a light drizzle was starting. It stung her face and reminded her that her newborn son shouldn't be kept out in such weather.

Shivering, Elizabeth clutched her baby more closely to her, and, turning sharply away, she hurried to the pram parked near the church gate. The baby, peaceful now, still seemed to be smiling secretly to himself…

And an anxious Maria, watching unseen by the side of the church, also shivered as she remembered that day, twenty years ago, when she stood by a stranger's grave holding her baby just as her daughter had done…

Epilogue

2010

'Please come with me,' Elizabeth begged her son.

The tall, quiet man looked at her with those unfathomable dark eyes that reminded her so much of the first Edward. She was flushed and excited, looking so much younger than her fifty years. He hadn't the heart to refuse such a simple request on her birthday.

'Of course I will, Mum.'

They walked companionably together to the church a mile away. It was cold, as expected on New Year's Day, with a crisp bite to the air which heralded snow, so they walked briskly, keeping each other company without needing to speak. He knew exactly where they were heading. They had made this walk every year throughout his childhood, and he was sure she had continued her birthday tradition after he left home to go to university and then start work in a solicitor's office.

They turned into the churchyard and headed straight for the large white marble headstone bearing his name. Edward was still struck by the coincidence, not only of having the same names as this unknown old man, but of the fact that the name of the stranger who had been pulled from the terrible fire at Highwood Hall was the same as his mother's maiden name. When he was younger he had asked her about the coincidences and she had woven a fantastic story to feed his imagination.

His mother stopped and bent to rub the dirt from the marble with her woollen mitten. 'That's better,' she said, satisfied that the writing was clear again. Then she stiffened.

'Oh, Edward, can you see him? He's right there, look!'

Edward turned to look in the direction where his mother was pointing, although he didn't expect to see anything. He never had before. But her eyes were sparkling and she smiled as she took a step forward. It had started to snow and large soft flakes were drifting down silently.

For a moment he could see nothing – only a rubbish bag caught in a tree close to the church wall, which twisted and flapped in the wind. He shivered: it was too cold for them to be standing here if a snowstorm was coming.

'Mum, this is just one of your fancies…'

And then he saw him – a man about his own age, standing just a few feet away, his hands outstretched, a smile on his face and dark curly hair and deep brown eyes, just like his own. Edward rubbed his eyes and stared again. But there was nothing, just the bag caught in the tree, twisting and flapping in the wind, and the snowflakes falling, thicker and faster.

'Please, Mum, we need to go. We'll freeze standing here and Dad will be worried about us.'

His mother's face closed down again and, reluctantly, she agreed to retrace their steps. He tucked his arm through hers as they turned to go. As they walked towards the church gates, he could hear a voice whispering behind them. 'Elizabeth, Elizabeth, my love. Edward, my beloved son…'

He swung round sharply, but could see no one. Only the snowflakes, whirling and dancing above the old man's grave…

ABOUT THE AUTHOR

Rosemary Hillyard's earliest memories are of wanting to be a writer. As Charles Dickens was an ancestor, perhaps the desire was in her genes! At the age of seven, she would be placed on a chair at primary school to make up stories to keep her classmates quiet, and at ten she won an all-London children's prize for a story about the work of the RSPCA.

By the time she reached her teens, too many adults had told Rosemary she needed to earn a living and keep story writing as a spare-time interest. So she trained as a journalist with her local paper in South London and stuck to factual writing for the next twenty-five years. An editor at one job told her, 'You'll never manage to write fiction while you spend every day writing factual news items and articles.'

He was right. Getting work in journalism became more difficult as Rosemary grew older, and in her forties she trained as a financial adviser, moving on to running her own business as an independent mortgage consultant.

The spur to start writing imaginatively came in the

form of therapy when her father died from cancer at the early age of fifty-eight.

The germ of an idea for a historical romance with the central character stepping back into history started to take shape and grow. But the need to earn a living throughout her life always came first, and it was never the right time for *A Time to Be...* to see the light of day.

Rosemary has now retired, and lives in a small village in Northern Ireland with John, her partner of twenty-five years. And at last, sixty years after she first dreamed of being a writer, her dream is coming true.